mary-kate olsen ashley olsen

so little time

Check out these other great
so little time
titles:

Book 1: **how to train a boy**

Book 2: **instant boyfriend**

Book 3: **too good to be true**

Book 4: **just between us**

Book 5: **tell me about it**

Book 6: **secret crush**

Coming soon!

Book 8: **the love factor**

mary-kate olsen   ashley olsen

so little time

girl talk

By Megan Stine

Based on the teleplay by Eric Cohen

HarperEntertainment
An *Imprint of* HarperCollins*Publishers*

A PARACHUTE PRESS BOOK

A PARACHUTE PRESS BOOK

Parachute Publishing, L.L.C.
156 Fifth Avenue, Suite 302
New York, NY 10010

Published by
≝HarperEntertainment
An *Imprint of* HarperCollins*Publishers*
10 East 53rd Street, New York, NY 10022-5299

First printing: January 2003

Printed in the United States of America

Visit HarperEntertainment on the World Wide Web at
www.harpercollins.com

10 9 8 7 6 5 4 3 2 1

chapter
one

"**W**here *is* it?" fourteen-year-old Riley Carlson mumbled to herself as she dug around in her dresser drawer. Her cute new peasant blouse had to be in there somewhere.

"Hmmm?" her twin sister, Chloe, answered absent-mindedly.

"I can't find it anywhere," Riley muttered, still digging. She had cut off the tags and ironed the top last night so she could wear it today. "Have you seen it, Chloe?"

"Seen what?" Chloe asked.

"My peasant blouse," Riley said. "I'm almost positive I put it right here. In this drawer."

"You mean the really cute one with the red and yellow flowers?" Chloe said.

"Yeah! That's it!" Riley whirled around, so happy her sister had found it. Then her mouth dropped open. "You're *wearing* it!"

"Yup. Thanks!" Chloe pushed her wavy blond hair behind her ears and bounced out of their bedroom. "See you later. Don't forget about debate club this afternoon," she called over her shoulder.

"Hey! Wait," Riley cried, running to stop her.

Too late. Chloe was already down the stairs and halfway out of the house.

"I don't believe it," Riley muttered as she sifted through her closet for something else to wear.

[<u>Riley</u>: Now, normally I wouldn't make such a big deal over a stupid shirt. But, you see, Chloe and I have this rule: No borrowing new clothes until the owner has worn them at least once. Oh, and guess who made up that rule. Chloe!]

Riley searched her side *and* Chloe's side of the closet. There wasn't another clean top in sight—except for the purple stretchy one she'd worn on Monday.

Oh well, she thought, pulling it on over her head. Today is Friday. Maybe no one will remember.

She slipped on her sneakers with the purple stripes, grabbed her backpack, and headed off for West Malibu High.

"Riley!" Sierra Pomeroy called as Riley hurried up the front steps. Sierra was one of Riley's coolest friends. She was the lead singer and bass guitar player in a rock band called The Wave.

"Hey," Riley said, joining Sierra. "What's up?"

"Don't even ask me why I have these bags under my eyes," Sierra replied as they entered the school. "I was up all night finishing a paper for English *and* writing a new bass line for a song. Hey, didn't you wear that purple thing on Monday?"

Riley rolled her eyes. "Look who's talking," she said, staring at Sierra's clothes. The girl was wearing the same plaid skirt and white blouse that she'd worn to school every single day that week.

"That's different," Sierra said. She hurried into the girls' rest room and pulled a scrunchie out of her hair. "I just haven't changed yet." Her wild wavy red hair fell down around her shoulders. She instantly looked ten times cooler.

Okay, she has a point, Riley thought. Sierra's real name was Sarah, and everyone on the planet knew she was leading a double life. Well, everyone except her parents.

They didn't want Sierra wearing the latest fashions. And they didn't want her to play bass guitar in a rock band. So she just didn't tell them about either one.

"The bell's going to ring soon," Riley said, checking her watch.

"No problem," Sierra said. "I've got this down to a three-minute event."

She pulled off the boring white blouse and stuffed it into her backpack. Quickly, she slipped into a black T-shirt with lace sleeves. Then she slid off the plaid skirt and pulled on a pair of stretchy black Capri pants.

"Done!" Sierra announced.

"Your mom must think we have school uniforms, the way you're dressing these days," Riley joked.

"I know!" Sierra laughed. "Can you believe it? And every day she says to me, 'Sarah, you look so nice today'! I don't even think she notices it's the same dumb skirt, over and over."

Funny, Riley thought. Sierra's mom was nice, but she *was* a little dense sometimes.

"Hey, you want to hang at California Dream after school?" Sierra asked.

"Can't," Riley said. "I mean, not until later, anyway. Chloe and I are joining the debate club today."

"Debate club?" Sierra wrinkled her nose. "How come?"

Riley shrugged. "Chloe asked me if I wanted to do it, and I said 'Why not?' Who knows? It might be fun."

"So I'll meet you after," Sierra said, entering a bathroom stall.

"Fine." Riley nodded. "I'll be there around four." She checked her watch again. "Gotta go."

Riley left the girls' rest room and pushed her way through the crowded halls toward her homeroom. She spotted Chloe talking to her friend Quinn Reyes and a cute boy near a row of lockers. As she got closer, she realized the guy was a freshman named Eric something.

"That's an awesome top you're wearing," Eric was saying when Riley joined the group.

"Yeah," Quinn agreed. "Love the hippie-chick thing you've got going on."

Riley smiled. After all, it was *her* top that was being admired. And any second now, Chloe was going to come clean about it.

"Thanks, you guys!" Chloe beamed.

Riley stared at her sister, waiting for her to say something else. Chloe wouldn't take the compliment without giving Riley the credit, would she?

A few seconds passed. I guess she would, Riley decided.

"Hey, Riley," Chloe said, "can you meet me outside the debate club room today?"

"Sure, but why?" Riley asked.

"So we can walk in together," Chloe said. "Otherwise we might both get stuck with some geeky guy as a debate partner."

"Okay," Riley said. Besides, she'd rather be teamed up with Chloe, anyway.

"Great," Chloe said. She whirled around and grabbed her biology book from her locker.

"Awesome top, Chloe!" Amanda Gray, another friend of Chloe's, called from the other side of the hall.

"Thanks, Amanda!" Chloe said over her shoulder.

She did it *again*. Riley frowned. She glanced at her sister to see if she'd even acknowledge that *Riley's* blouse was getting all of the compliments.

Then the bell rang and Riley had to go.

Well...it's just a shirt, Riley reminded herself. No big deal. And it does look great on Chloe, which means it's going to look fabulous on me, too. That is, if I ever get to wear it!

Riley leaned against a wall outside the debate club room, peeking inside every thirty seconds. The meeting was just about to start. Where was Chloe?

I hate to be late, Riley thought, trying to decide whether to go in without her sister. No, she thought. Chloe specifically asked me to wait. I'll stay here a few more minutes.

Finally Chloe came running up. "Sorry!" she explained quickly. "Mr. Cooksey kept me after class to talk about my make-up test. You should have gone in without me."

"But I thought you said—" Riley began, then stopped. Forget it, she thought. It's not worth even saying it.

They hurried inside.

Mr. Woolrich, the debate club adviser, was pacing around at the front of the classroom, giving instructions to the group.

"Oh, Chloe and Riley," he greeted them. "Glad you decided to come. Um, we've already chosen partners for the next debate, but you two could work together if you'd like."

Perfect! Riley thought. That's just what they'd had in mind, anyway.

"Or one of you can work with Eric Dooley," Mr. Woolrich added.

"I'll be Eric's partner," Chloe volunteered quickly.

Riley's mouth fell open. Was she kidding?

"But, Chloe," Riley whispered, "who am I supposed to be partners with?"

"But Eric is *soooo* cute!" Chloe whispered. "Come on. Please. You don't mind, do you? *Pleeeeeeease*?"

"Fine," Riley said. But inside, her stomach turned into a knot. She did mind. A lot.

[<u>Riley</u>: **Okay, I'm taking a poll. Would YOU do that to YOUR sister? Well, I wouldn't—no matter how cute the guy was!**]

"Thanks, Riles!" Chloe didn't seem to notice the angry look on Riley's face. She headed for the empty seat next to Eric.

Riley just stood there for a minute. No, thank *you*, she wanted to say. Thanks for nothing!

Mr. Woolrich laughed gently. "Well, take a seat, anyway, Riley," he said. "Maybe you can pair up with another team as an alternate. You could step in if someone gets sick."

For half a second Riley thought about leaving. Why stay if she couldn't even be part of a debate? But everyone was staring, waiting for her to sit down, so she sat.

Mr. Woolrich cleared his throat and began to pace the room again. "For those of you who are new, we do things a little differently in this debate club," he said.

Riley zoned out, only half listening. Why bother? She wasn't going to be debating anyone. Then she spotted Larry entering the classroom.

Larry Slotnick, the boy who lived next door to Riley and Chloe. Larry, who had been so in love with Riley for years that he would fall all over himself whenever he would see her.

Correction: He *used to* fall all over himself. Now he was dating Sierra—which was great, as far as Riley was concerned. Larry and Sierra had been going out for a couple of weeks.

Larry was sweet and a good friend. But normally, Riley wouldn't have been too excited to see him.

Until now.

"Larry!" She almost leaped out of her seat. She'd never been so happy to see anyone in her whole life. Larry could be her debate partner!

"Larry, are you joining us?" Mr. Woolrich asked.

"I guess so," Larry said.

"Good," Mr. Woolrich replied. "You can be Riley's team partner. You two will go up against Chloe and Eric since the four of you are the least experienced."

"Okay," Larry said, sounding kind of nervous. He started to put his books on a desk but missed. The whole stack hit the floor.

"What's wrong?" Riley whispered as he took a seat beside her.

"My parents are making me do this debate stuff," Larry explained. "I'm totally freaked out about it."

"Making you do it? How come?" Riley asked.

"I guess they want me to get over my fear of public speaking." He shivered. "I hate getting up in front of people. It makes me feel like I'm on that TV show *Fear Factor*. You know, the one where contestants have to confront their worst fears to win fifty thousand bucks? I'm going home a loser, Riley. I just know it."

Fear Factor? Uh-oh. Maybe Larry wasn't exactly the best partner. But who cared? At least she *had* a partner.

"Hey, don't worry," she said, trying to cheer him up. "I used to be afraid to get up in front of people. But I got over it, and you can, too."

"Do you really think so?" Larry asked.

"You bet," she said. "You'll be fine. I'll help you."

"You will?" Larry looked really grateful.

"Of course!" Riley promised. "Meet me at California Dream later and we'll practice. By the time we're through, fear definitely won't be a factor for you anymore. Just wait and see!"

chapter
two

"**M**mmm. What's that smell?" Chloe asked as she burst into the living room after school. "Wait. Don't tell me." She closed her eyes and took a deep whiff.

Manuelo, the housekeeper-slash-cook, was sitting on a chair in the living room. He had been practically a member of the family for years—especially now that Chloe and Riley's parents were separated. Now the girls lived in the beach house with their mother while their dad lived in a trailer park nearby.

[Chloe: So why is my father staying in a dinky trailer when Mom, Riley, and I are in a fancy beach house? Well, Dad explains it like this: He's trying to find himself. And how can he do that if he's living in luxury? I say, how can you find yourself if you're not? But it works for him, so I guess it's okay.]

"Manuelo, you made your famous fried mushrooms!" Chloe cried. She hurried into the kitchen and brought a plate of them into the living room.

"Take a few and put the rest back, Chloe," Manuelo said, waving his hand. "Tedi is trying very hard not to even smell them!"

Tedi, a gorgeous, tall, dark-skinned model, was slumped on the living room couch. She modeled all the clothes for Chloe's mom, Macy, who was a fashion designer.

"Wrong," Tedi said, taking a deep breath. "Smell is all I'm allowed to do, so I'm totally into it. What else are we smelling today?"

"Well, if you stick around long enough we'll be smelling homemade veggie pizza with extra cheese," Manuelo admitted.

"Ohhhh." Tedi closed her eyes and moaned.

Chloe checked out the outfit Tedi was wearing. It was a cute pair of low-rise paisley Capri pants with a matching orange and pink top. Even in her slumped position, her bare midriff was so flat, you could write a term paper on it.

What's she worried about? Chloe wondered.

"Tedi, you can't starve yourself," she said, popping a mushroom into her mouth. She passed the plate to the model. "Go on, have one. You've got to eat to stay healthy."

"She's also got to try on string bikinis as soon as

your mother gets home," Manuelo said, taking the plate. "I'm putting these back in the kitchen."

"He's right—unfortunately," Tedi complained as Manuelo left the room. "I'm not supposed to eat fried or greasy foods. I can't go to the beach and swim in the ocean because the sun and saltwater are bad for my hair. I've got to fly all over the world, so I'm constantly jet-lagged. I have absolutely zero time to myself. And even if I didn't, my agent won't let me do anything fun like in-line skating or windsurfing because I might fall and get an ugly bruise."

Chloe shook her head. "That's crazy, Tedi. You should be able to do what you want. What's the point of being a successful model if you can't enjoy life?"

"Totally," Tedi agreed. "I mean, it's a beautiful day outside, and the ocean is right there!" She pointed through the sliding glass doors, past the deck, to the water. "I should be able to go outside and enjoy it. Instead, I'm stuck in the house all day, waiting for Macy to do fittings. And I'm starving!"

Chloe picked up a bowl of fruit from the coffee table. "Want a peach or something?"

"No!" Tedi cried. "I want a milk shake!"

"Then have one," Chloe said. "A milk shake once in a while won't hurt. And take some time off, too. You deserve it! Hang out with your friends. Go in the ocean—even if the saltwater *is* bad for your hair. You have to have some balance in your life, Tedi. You can't work twenty-four/seven."

"You are *so* right!" Tedi stood up and headed for the door. "I'm going out for a milk shake. And I'm not going to let anyone stop me!"

"But—" Chloe watched as Tedi breezed through the front door. It banged closed. "I didn't mean *right now*."

Wow, Chloe thought, stunned. If I can talk Tedi into blowing off her diet, then I can probably talk anyone into *anything*.... Cool. Eric and I are going to *rock* in the West Malibu High debate!

"Wait, wait, wait. Chloe did *what*?" Sierra asked, setting down her mocha and pushing her books aside.

Riley and Sierra had just slipped into a booth at California Dream, their favorite beach hangout. Riley glanced out at the ocean, then back at Sierra.

"Well, for one, she wore my new shirt today without asking me," Riley said. "I mean, my *brand-new* shirt. I've never even worn it. And two, she asked me to join the debate team with her and then she didn't pick me to be her partner! She teamed up with Eric instead."

"Okay, that's totally unforgivable." Sierra paused. "Unless she has a good reason. Who's Eric?"

"Cute freshman. Dark hair, blue eyes, Ultimate Frisbee team," Riley said.

Sierra nodded. "Well, that's a good reason...but not good enough to leave you without a partner. You think she has another excuse?"

"I doubt it," Riley said.

"But you don't know for sure until you talk to her," Sierra said. "Just ask her about it. Don't let it build up into a whole thing. That would be the worst."

Riley considered what Sierra was saying. But she also knew that if she *did* talk to Chloe, they might wind up getting into a fight over it, and Riley didn't want that to happen. She and her sister practically *never* fought!

"I'll think about it," she said slowly, "but first I've got to figure out a way to help Larry get over his public-speaking freak-out."

Sierra laughed. "Good luck."

"What does that mean?" Riley asked. "You're going out with the guy. Shouldn't you be more...I don't know...supportive?"

"Oh, I'm supportive," Sierra said. "I mean, Larry's awesome. But I know how nervous he can get. I don't see why his parents are making him do this, anyway."

"I know," Riley said. "It seems like cruel and unusual punishment to torture him like that. Making him get up in front of people when he's terrified."

"Totally," Sierra agreed. "It's sort of like making someone who's afraid of heights join the rock-climbing team." She tilted her head. "Or like making someone who's afraid of short skirts join the cheerleading squad."

Riley laughed. "Anyway, the worst part is, he and I are up against Chloe." She took a sip of her mocha. "That's going to be weird."

"Hey, my two favorite girls are here!" Larry cried as

he walked in the front door. He knocked over two chairs on his way across the room to join them.

"And Riley," he said, shaking his head and gazing at her. "I must say, you look totally amazing with a mocha mustache."

Don't tell me that! Riley thought. She grabbed for a napkin.

Larry burst out laughing. "Just kidding," he said. "But honestly, Riley—you *would* look great with a mocha mustache. You look fantastic no matter what you do."

"Yeah," Sierra teased. "Let me know when you decide to grow a mustache. So I can take pictures and sell them to the carnival."

"Shut up!" Riley smiled and gave Sierra a little push.

Larry laughed, too. "Isn't Sierra funny, Riley?" He gave Sierra one of his lovesick smiles, and she stared into his eyes, smiling back.

"So are we going to work on your public-speaking skills?" Riley asked.

Larry nodded. "Maybe you can *both* help me," he said, glancing from Riley to Sierra and back again.

Sierra shook her head and nudged Larry to let her out of the booth. "No way. I'm not that patient. Besides, I've got to kick it to a band rehearsal," she said. "You two have fun."

"Say hi to Alex," Riley called as Sierra headed for the door. "Tell him I'll call him tonight."

Alex Zimmer was Riley's boyfriend and the lead guitarist in Sierra's band.

Larry wriggled back into the booth and finished off Sierra's mocha. "Okay, where do we start?" he asked.

Good question. Riley thought for a minute. Their debate topic was why homeless people should be allowed to sleep in public spaces.

Riley hadn't really thought out all the arguments, but they were supposed to take the pro side, in favor.

"Just start with some kind of opening statement," she said. "Say something like: 'There are no good reasons why homeless people should not be allowed to sleep in train stations or in libraries.' And then go on from there."

"Okay." Larry nodded and pulled himself up straight. He folded his hands in front of him, as if he was standing at a lectern. He took a deep breath. "There are no good reasons why homeless people should not be allowed to...to..."

He glanced around the room and seemed to get a little nervous.

"...to sleep in train stations, heh-heh-heh," he said with a little giggle.

"Larry!" Riley whispered. "You've got to focus. Try to concentrate."

"Okay, okay." He nodded.

Riley checked out the room to see if anyone was watching them. Larry's giggle was sort of high-pitched. It made him sound like a maniac. "Start over, okay?" she said, trying to be encouraging.

Larry cleared his throat and put on a straight face. "There's no good reason..." he began. But then he cracked a smile. "...no g-g-good reason why...heh-heh-heh!" He giggled.

"Shh!" Riley glanced over her shoulder. A bunch of seniors were staring at them as if they were junior high kids who didn't know how to act in public.

"I can't help it," Larry said, still giggling. "I told you I get nervous."

"That's okay, we'll just keep working at it," Riley said. "But try to be serious. We're talking about *homeless* people here. It's not funny—remember that."

Larry sat up and tried to look serious. "Okay, here goes," he said firmly. "There is no reason why homeless people—"

As soon as he said "homeless people," he cackled again. By the time he reached the end of the sentence, he was laughing so hard, he was crying.

Oh, man, Riley thought, covering her face with her hands. Curing Larry was going to be tougher than she'd thought!

chapter
three

We *seriously* need to do laundry, Chloe decided as she stared into her closet Saturday morning. There's nothing to wear. Absolutely *nothing*.

Riley was already up and out of bed, and she seemed to have taken the last cute pair of pants in the house.

Where is Riley, anyway? Chloe wondered, padding downstairs to grab some orange juice and yogurt.

She hadn't seen her sister since debate club yesterday afternoon. Apparently Riley had hung out with Larry last night and Chloe was already asleep by the time Riley had gotten home.

Chloe noticed Pepper's leash was missing from its hook in the kitchen. Uh-oh. Riley was out walking the puppy again, even though it was Chloe's turn.

She's going to be cranky when she gets back, Chloe thought. She felt really guilty, but she still wanted to get out of the house before Riley could bug her about it.

She finished her yogurt and hurried back upstairs to get dressed. With the pile of dirty clothes on the closet floor and another pile stuffed under Riley's bed, there weren't many cutting-edge fashion choices left. She was rummaging around on her side of the closet when the phone rang.

Chloe grabbed the phone, hoping it was someone interesting. "Hello?"

"Hey," Alex said on the other end of the line. "Is Riley there?"

"She's out walking Pepper," Chloe said. "Do you want to leave a message?"

"Uh...yeah," Alex said, sort of slowly, as if he wasn't sure what to say. "Um...on second thought, just tell her to call me."

"You got it," Chloe said and hung up. The minute she put it down, the phone rang again. "Yeah?" she answered, thinking it was Alex again.

"Hi," Tedi said. "Is this Chloe or Riley? I can't tell you apart over the phone."

"It's me, Chloe," she said. "What's up? You want to talk to my mom? Because I think she's at her Saturday morning spin class or something."

"No, no, no, I was calling you," Tedi said. "Remember how you said yesterday that I should take some time for myself once in a while? Have fun? Hang with my friends?"

"Yeah." Chloe nodded. "So?"

"So I don't *have* any friends!" Tedi moaned. "I mean, how could I? I never do anything but model! I am so, so, *sooo* bored. Do you want to do something? Maybe go to the mall?"

Go to the mall with a supermodel? Go shopping with just about the coolest, most fashionable person she knew?

"Definitely!" Chloe leaped at the chance.

"Good," Tedi said. "I'm in the neighborhood. I'll pick you up in fifteen minutes."

Chloe hung up and showered quickly. Then she hurried to see if her hair was going to give her problems today.

No, it was okay. Her long blond hair was just wavy enough. She arranged some of the best curls so they'd sort of hang by her face and look pretty. Then she turned back to the closet. There still wasn't a thing to wear.

Laundry for sure tonight! she promised herself.

She pulled on her only remaining clean pair of jeans. The problem was something to wear on top. The only thing that would look even remotely right was the same top she'd worn yesterday—Riley's peasant blouse.

Might as well, she decided. I mean, it's not really clean anymore, so Riley probably won't want to wear it herself, anyway.

And besides—Chloe had a cute little red shoulder bag that would look awesome with it. Red sandals pulled the whole outfit together.

Now the makeup, Chloe thought. She couldn't go

shopping with a supermodel unless her makeup was fabulous!

She put on lip liner, gloss, blush, and eye shadow. But she still needed something else. Maybe a little eyeliner.

Too bad mine's worn down to the end of the pencil, she thought. Oh well. She'd just have to borrow Riley's. She won't mind, Chloe decided. We borrow each other's stuff all the time, anyway.

She checked the mirror twice more after she heard Tedi's car outside. Tedi was waiting in her white Miata convertible with the top down.

"Hi!" Chloe called and climbed into the passenger seat. Then she sort of gasped. Tedi had on an old pair of jeans with a sweatshirt that looked like something you'd wear to a school car wash.

"Aren't we going shopping?" She stared at Tedi's clothes.

Tedi pulled away from the curb. "Yeah. Why?" Then she caught the look in Chloe's eyes. "Oh, this." She glanced down at her outfit. "I never dress up when I'm out in public. It's bad enough that people mob me for autographs when I just throw on some old thing."

Ohhh, Chloe thought. Right.

"And besides, I'm not a supermodel today!" Tedi announced happily. She turned into the mall parking lot. "I'm just a regular person—so I don't have to look great."

"I thought it was the other way around," Chloe

mumbled. "I mean, I thought ordinary mortals like me had to work really hard to look great, while supermodels like you could just slack off since you already look amazing all the time."

Tedi laughed, parked the car, and they hurried into the mall.

"This is the best!" Tedi said. They rode the escalator to the second level. "I mean it. I haven't been in a mall in months. Of course, when I was a model, I didn't have to go out looking for clothes. They came looking for me."

"What do you mean *when you were a model*?" Chloe asked. "You haven't quit. You're just taking some time for yourself. Right?"

"Wrong," Tedi announced. "I'm sick of the whole thing. I'm not going to do it anymore."

Whoa. Give up modeling? Chloe tried to wrap her mind around that idea. "But how come?" she asked as they browsed a new store window.

"It's what you said yesterday," Tedi explained. "I should be allowed to drink a milk shake. Or go to the beach once in a while." She walked into the store.

Chloe followed her. "But you could do those things *and* be a supermodel," she argued.

"No way," Tedi said. "I took your advice. I just want to be an average person like you. No offense," she added really quickly.

Chloe didn't know if she should be offended or not. She decided on not.

"Hey! This would look incredible on you," Tedi said, grabbing a tiny black leather skirt off the rack.

"I know," Chloe said. "It does. I already have it."

Tedi laughed, and they left the store. Then she grabbed Chloe's arm. "Uh-oh, look out. Here they come." She nodded toward a bunch of high school girls who seemed to be marching straight toward them. "Autograph time," Tedi said, sighing and then pretending to give in.

The five girls were smiling and rushing toward them. But then they just kept going, past Chloe and Tedi, not stopping.

"Hi!" one of them called to a group of about six high school guys behind them.

Tedi whirled around and then sort of laughed at her own mistake. "Oh. Okay. So I guess they *weren't* going to mob me," she said. "Thank goodness!"

Weird, Chloe thought. She *sounds* happy, but she looks kind of disappointed.

Tedi glanced in a mirror as she passed it and suddenly started changing her hair. It had been twisted on top of her head. When she let it down, she looked ten times more glamorous.

I'll bet she *wanted* those girls to recognize her, Chloe realized. She's totally bummed that they didn't!

But Chloe didn't blame her. Wasn't that half the fun of being a supermodel?

That's why she'll never really quit, Chloe decided.

"Ooh, check out this place!" Tedi said as she slipped into the next store, a cute boutique called Top Down. She glided through the store, fingering half the clothes on the racks. Chloe could barely keep up with her.

"What about this?" Tedi yanked another little skirt off the rack. "This would be amazing with that shirt you're wearing."

"Awesome! It's my size—and it's on sale, too!" Chloe noticed.

"So buy it!" Tedi ordered her.

Should she? Chloe wasn't sure. Wasn't it sort of wrong to buy a skirt to go with one of *Riley's* tops?

"You've *got* to have it," Tedi urged her. "It's perfect!"

"But this isn't my top," Chloe admitted. "It's Riley's."

"So then *she'll* borrow the skirt!" Tedi said as if it was the most obvious thing in the world.

Okay, Chloe thought. Why not? Maybe I'll even let Riley wear it first. It would look great on her.

She bought the skirt and let Tedi pick out a great pair of shoes to go with it. Then they got soft pretzels and lemonade in the food court before heading home.

On their way out of the mall, Tedi bought a scarf and showed Chloe how to wrap it around her head. It sort of looked like a cross between a bandanna and a scrunchie, and it made Chloe's hair look totally fabulous.

"I learned that on a fashion shoot in the Bahamas," Tedi mentioned, "when one of the girls got her hair wet by mistake."

"It is so cool to be a model," Chloe gushed.

"I thought you were on *my* side!" Tedi snapped. "If it's so cool, then why am I quitting?"

Why are you? Chloe wondered as they drove home.

[Chloe: The way I see it, Tedi's just going through some sort of midlife crisis. Except can you have a midlife crisis when you're only twenty-four? Weird! Actually, I guess you can be any age when you get a big jolt and suddenly see something clearly for the first time. It happened to me when I was six. Mr. Rogers was on TV, and I suddenly realized that watching a middle-aged guy put on a sweater was NOT fun. Well, not as fun as watching a yellow bird do the funky chicken. Anyway, I figure Tedi will get over this crisis eventually. I mean, I got over mine when I was ten. Everyone knows that Mr. Rogers rocks!]

Chloe hopped out of the Miata and bounced into the house with her shopping bags swinging from her arm.

"Hi, hi!" she called to her mom and Manuelo, who were sitting in the living room with their arms folded across their chests and staring at each other.

[Chloe: Hold it. Did I say just sitting in the living room staring at each other? Uh-oh. That's not normal—not for my mom. She's always running from one thing to another. Even when she's

sleeping! You should see it. Her feet move in her
sleep just like Pepper does when she's dreaming
about running. No, this is weird. Something's up.]

"Mom? Manuelo? What's wrong?" Chloe asked,
dropping her packages and walking into the living room.

Her mother glanced up. "Was that Tedi's car I just
saw pulling away?" she asked in a glum tone.

Chloe nodded. "Why?"

"Oh, we're just wondering why you're hanging out
with the enemy," Manuelo said in his thick Hispanic
accent.

"Tedi's not the enemy," Chloe protested. "She's our
friend! Why would you be angry with her? Just because
she wants to have a little fun once in a while?"

"No," Manuelo said. "Because she decided to quit
modeling one week before your mother's big show!"

Chloe's heart skipped a beat. "Tedi mentioned
something about quitting, but I didn't think she'd actually *do* it," she said, her voice thin.

"Well, she did," Macy announced. "And now I'm in
deep trouble. The biggest fashion show of the year is
next Friday!"

"Can't you get another model?" Chloe asked.

Macy glanced up and shot Chloe a sad but understanding look. "No, honey, I can't. For one thing, all the
important clothes have been custom-fit to Tedi. And for
another thing, even if I wanted someone else to head-
line my show, all the top models are already booked. It's

Fashion Week. Every serious designer on the West Coast has been planning this for months."

Oh, no, Chloe thought. She had no idea her mother's show depended so much on Tedi! This was a disaster, and it was all Chloe's fault. If she hadn't talked Tedi into taking some time for herself, this never would have happened.

Chloe swallowed hard. There was only one thing to do. She had to get Tedi back into modeling before Mom's show.

But how?

chapter
four

"**A**nother latte?" the waitress at California Dream asked Riley as she passed by her table.

Riley checked her watch. It was 11:45 on Saturday morning. Alex was supposed to be there forty-five minutes ago. But there was no sign of him yet.

"No thanks." Riley shook her head. "I'm good."

"Okay. But you've got a latte mustache on your lip," the waitress said.

"That's not funny," Riley muttered. And what was up with that? Now the *waitresses* were doing Larry's joke material?

She glanced out the window toward the ocean. The sun had just moved, so she could see her own reflection in the window glass. She noticed a thin line of foamed milk right across her upper lip.

Ahh! I *do* have a latte mustache! she realized, grabbing for a napkin.

Today was definitely not her day. First she'd awakened in a sweat, from a nightmare about the debate with Larry. In the dream he not only giggled the whole time, he drooled, too.

Then she had to take out the dog because Chloe wouldn't get up. And after Riley got back from running Pepper on the beach, there was no yogurt left. Chloe had finally gotten up, eaten the last one, and left!

The girl was really beginning to get on her nerves!

Now Alex was late for their date. And that wasn't like him. Usually Alex was really considerate. He was the best boyfriend she'd ever had.

[Riley: Okay, okay. So he's the ONLY boyfriend I've ever had. He's still awesome.]

So where was he? He had promised to meet her here when they talked on the phone last night. They were going to brainstorm some kind of plan to help Larry with his fear of public speaking.

I can't wait much longer, she thought. She had to get to Larry's house soon.

The door opened and Riley spotted Tara Jordan poking her head in. She was one of Chloe's good friends.

"Hi," Riley said, waving from her booth.

Tara bounced over to her. "I'm not staying," she reported. "I was just checking out the scene, but of course no one's ever here Saturday morning. What's up?"

"I'm meeting Alex, but he's late," Riley complained. "Can I borrow your cell?"

Tara pulled her phone out of her bag and handed it over.

"Thanks." Riley dialed Alex at home. "Alex? Where are you?" she asked when he picked up. "I've been sitting in California Dream for almost an hour."

"Didn't Chloe tell you?" Alex sounded upset. "I called this morning to cancel, but you were out with the dog or something. I told her to tell you to call me. I tried calling again, but nobody was home."

Unbelievable! Riley thought.

"Chloe didn't give me the message," she said, starting to fume. She tried to keep her voice calm. After all, it wasn't Alex's fault that her sister was so inconsiderate! "What happened? Why can't you come?"

"My uncle showed up in town to surprise my mom," Alex explained. "We haven't seen him in four years, so I've got to hang around. Family time."

That's fair, Riley thought. But she was still kind of disappointed.

"Can we talk later? I'm really freaked out about this Larry thing. I have no idea how to get him to stop laughing, and I really want to do well in the debate," she said.

"Yeah, for sure," Alex said. "Sorry."

He was so sweet! He really sounded honestly sorry, Riley thought.

"I'll call you tonight," Alex said before they hung up.

"Thanks." Riley handed the phone back to Tara and headed off to Larry's house.

Riley thought about Alex as she walked there. How many girls have a boyfriend like that? Most of the freshman guys at West Malibu were...well...

Actually, most of them were more like Larry. Nice guys who just didn't have a clue about how to act around girls.

Larry opened his front door when she rang the bell. He had something white across his upper lip.

"Larry, what's on your face?" she asked him.

"A smile because I'm always happy to see you?" he guessed.

"No, on your lip."

Larry felt his upper lip with his finger. "Is it a yogurt mustache?"

"How do you get yogurt on your upper lip?" she asked.

"I like to suck it out of the container in one whole slurp," he said with a silly grin.

[Riley: Ever feel as if your life is like a bad sitcom?
Oh. Um, me neither. I was just wondering....]

"Whatever." Riley shook her head. "Let's just get busy, okay?" She marched into his living room and sat down. "Did you make any notes about our debate topic?"

"I did," Larry said.

Wow. Riley wasn't expecting that answer. He was actually taking it seriously!

"Okay, that's good," she said, relaxing a little.

"I thought maybe if I spent some time thinking about the topic and really got into it, I wouldn't laugh so much when I'm up onstage," Larry explained.

"Excellent!" Riley nodded in approval. "So do you want to start? Just stand up and tell me what you have to say."

Riley sat back on the couch and folded her hands. She put a "listening" expression on her face so that Larry would think of her as an audience, not just as Riley.

Larry cleared his throat and stood in front of her. He opened his mouth to start but then didn't.

"It's okay," Riley said. "Don't think about it. Just go for it."

Larry cleared his throat again. "Uh, the thing is, it's just plain wrong to make people feel bad about being homeless by telling them they can't sleep in a library," he said. "I mean, think about it. They already know they're homeless. So if you kick them out of the library, then they're library-less, too. Right?" He giggled a little.

Riley rolled her eyes. "Whoa, whoa, whoa," she said, putting her hands up. "Don't go there. I mean it, Larry. If you start making dumb jokes, of course you're going to laugh."

"But isn't that right? Aren't they library-less *and* homeless?" Larry insisted.

"Larry, you're going to be *friendless* if you don't take this seriously!" Riley said.

"Okay," he said, forcing a serious expression onto his face. "I'll try again."

"Just concentrate on your notes," Riley said. "Don't think about anything else."

Larry nodded, and for two hours they worked hard on the debate topic. At first he laughed and goofed off. But by the time they'd gone over the same stuff for the zillionth time, he knew it with his eyes closed.

He stood in front of Riley with a completely straight face. He even had an air of confidence by now. And he made a totally convincing argument.

Riley listened with her mouth open, stunned.

"...And so I conclude by saying that it's not just our duty as citizens but our duty as human beings to allow homeless people to make their homes wherever they can," Larry said at the end. "In the parks, the libraries, or the train stations. If we deny them this, we deny them the most basic of rights—the right to live on this earth." He folded his hands at the end and smiled.

"That was amazing!" Riley said. "You made a really great argument—and you didn't laugh once!"

Larry nodded, proud of himself, while Riley looked through her debate notes.

"Honestly, Larry, that was fantastic," she went on. "You covered every point I was going to make!"

Larry beamed. "Thanks. And I didn't get nervous at all. You cured me, Riley!"

I did! Riley thought happily. I really did!

chapter
five

"**W**here are you going?" Larry followed Riley toward the door like a tagalong puppy.

"To my house," Riley announced. "We need to celebrate your big success! And I happen to know that Manuelo made some of his famous cheese things last night. We can nuke the leftovers as a reward for all your hard work."

"Great," Larry said. "But can I ask you a question? How come everything Manuelo makes is famous? I mean, you're always talking about his 'famous cheese things' or his 'famous baby pizzas' or his 'famous fried mushrooms.' Once I think you even mentioned his 'famous cereal and milk'!"

"He's so sensitive, we've got to keep him happy," Riley replied with a laugh. They entered the house and went straight to the kitchen.

While Riley was heating up the cheese things,

Manuelo came home with his arms full of groceries.

"Ohhh, you're eating my famous cheese things," he moaned, clapping a hand to his mouth.

"Is there a problem?" Riley asked.

"No, no," Manuelo said, gesturing for her to go ahead. "I just wanted to be here to see the look of total yummy satisfaction spread across your face."

"Well, you're not too late," Riley said. "Anyway, Larry deserves a treat. He's been working on his fear of public speaking and I think he's gotten over it."

"Let me see," Manuelo said.

"Huh?" Riley looked confused.

"Show me how you can speak in public," Manuelo urged Larry. He set the bags of groceries on the counter and crossed his arms, waiting. "I'll be your audience. Go ahead—debate me."

Riley laughed. "We aren't going to debate *you*, Manuelo," she said. "We're going to debate together, against other teams."

"Whatever." Manuelo waved his hand impatiently. "Just do it."

Okay, Riley thought. This will be a good test. She nodded to Larry to go ahead.

Larry cleared his throat and pulled himself up straight.

But Riley noticed that his hands were shaking and he looked a little panicky and pale.

Like maybe he was going to faint.

35

He cleared his throat again. "Uh, today my partner and I are going to prove that there is no justifiable reason for sleeping in homeless places."

Oh, no. Riley's heart sank. Was that the best he could do?

"Stay focused," Riley whispered to him. "Really. You can do it."

Larry tried to straighten up, but he was close to giggling. "Of course, I mean there's no reason why homeless people should be s-s-sleeping places..." He giggled more.

"Come on, Larry," Riley said, trying to pump him up. "Hang in there!"

She could see that Larry was really trying hard not to laugh, but the corners of his mouth were already crinkling into a smile.

"Today, my partner and I are going explain the rights of the public who-who-who-who sleep in people's homes...ha-ha-ha-ha-ha!"

"This is *after* he got over his fear of public speaking?" Manuelo asked Riley.

Riley shrugged and looked helplessly at Larry. He was all-out laughing like a hyena now.

"Because if this is Larry without fear," Manuelo continued, "my advice to you is: Be afraid. Be very afraid!"

"Tara? It's me," Chloe said into the phone. She was in her room, lying back on her bed with her feet on the wall. "Listen, you've got to help me."

"What's up?" Tara asked.

Tons, Chloe thought. Where do I start?

For one thing, she really wanted to talk to Riley. It seemed as if Riley had something on her mind, but Chloe didn't know what it was—and Riley hardly seemed to be around lately.

For another, she was starting to worry about the upcoming debate. She hadn't done a thing to get ready, and she was supposed to be practicing with Eric tonight. But there was no way she could concentrate on that right now.

Mostly she was worried about the Tedi problem. She quickly explained the whole thing to Tara—about how Tedi had quit just when her mom needed her most.

"That's not *your* fault," Tara argued.

"But I feel totally responsible, anyway," Chloe said. "This is really big. And my mom's whole collection will be ruined if I don't do something."

"So come over!" Tara said. "Like, right now. Quinn's coming for a sleepover, and we can figure something out together."

"I can't," Chloe said. "I have to work on my debate with Eric in an hour. And then I promised Amanda I'd do something with her tonight if there was any time left."

"Cancel with Eric and tell Amanda to hang with us," Tara replied as if it was settled.

"Four people sleeping over? Like in junior high?" Chloe smiled.

"Bring a sleeping bag. It'll be fun!" Tara said.

"Can I bring a stuffed animal?" Chloe joked.

"You can bring a whole zoo for all I care," Tara said. "Just get over here. The worst that can happen is that we'll get bored, act like idiots, and eat too many chips."

Okay, yeah, Chloe thought. That was a plan. She could call Eric and reschedule. They still had plenty of time to work on their topic. Maybe they could do it tomorrow or sometime next week after school. The debate wasn't until Thursday, anyway.

And a girly night at Tara's sounded like fun! Between the four of them—Tara, Quinn, Amanda, and herself—they should be able to come up some kind of plan to help her mom, shouldn't they?

She hung up with Tara and dialed Eric's number.

"I'm sorry, he's not home yet," Eric's mother said. "He should be here any minute."

"I have to cancel our debate practice. Would you ask him to call me so we can set up another time?" Chloe asked.

"Sure," Mrs. Dooley said.

After the call, Chloe started to pack for the sleepover. When she finished packing, she called Amanda and filled her in on the plan.

I wish Riley could come, too, Chloe thought. She'd been dying to tell Riley all about the Tedi problem. They'd always solved this kind of crisis together.

But even when Riley *was* home, it seemed as if they

only passed each other in the kitchen. They hadn't said much to each other the whole day. Chloe made a mental note to ask Riley what she'd been up to as soon as she saw her tomorrow.

By the time Manuelo dropped her off at Tara's, Chloe was starved.

"My mom's out picking up Chinese food," Tara explained. "I'll get something for us to munch on while we're waiting."

Chloe tossed her backpack on the floor in Tara's room and opened her sleeping bag. Quinn and Amanda were already sprawled out on the floor.

"Okay, so what do we do?" Chloe asked after she had filled everyone in on the Tedi situation.

Quinn was playing with a lock of her hair, twisting it around her fingers. "Well, you've got to make Tedi think she's made a huge mistake by giving up modeling," she said.

"Obviously," Chloe said. "But how?"

"Maybe we could convince her that when models quit, they turn into freaky aliens or something," Quinn said, laughing.

Chloe rolled her eyes.

"Yeah! We write an article about it," Amanda said, getting into the spirit of things. "We make it look real—like it's a page off the Internet or something. And then we e-mail it to her!"

Amanda was Chloe's newest friend, and Chloe liked

her a lot. But she was still sort of quiet and shy, unlike Tara and Quinn.

"Ooh! That's good," Quinn said. "And my little brother has one of those photo-morphing programs on his computer. Maybe we could make a picture of Tedi where her skin is green and she has those creepy big black eyes. We'll send it with the article."

"I hope you guys aren't serious," Chloe said, even though she knew that they weren't.

"Hey, here's a crazy idea," Amanda said. "Why don't you just ask her to go back to modeling?"

"Nuh-uh," Chloe said, shaking her head. "Won't work. Tedi practically jumped down my throat when I told her how cool it was to be a model. She said she was following my advice and that I should be on *her* side."

Tara walked into her bedroom with a plate full of carrot sticks, raw cauliflower, snow peas, and blue cheese dip.

"Yummmm," Chloe said, dipping a carrot stick.

Amanda and Quinn grabbed some munchies, too.

"Any ideas?" Tara asked, nibbling on a snow pea pod.

"Nothing workable," Chloe reported.

Tara munched. Then her eyes lit up. "How about a fan club?"

"A fan club?" Chloe liked that idea.

"Yeah. We could get a whole bunch of people to, like, go up to Tedi and mob her or something," Tara explained.

"That might work," Chloe said, nodding. "We were at the mall this morning and she thought some girls were going to hound her for autographs. And when they didn't, she was totally bummed."

"Perfect," Tara said. "So we start the Tedi Fan Club. We'll put up a Web site or something, and—"

"But I don't get it," Amanda interrupted. "How will that make her want to go back to modeling? I mean, she only quit yesterday, so a fan club isn't going to do anything except show her that she's popular even if she *isn't* modeling."

Chloe frowned. What could she say? Amanda was right.

For the next two hours, they brainstormed. Amanda came up with the funniest idea. It involved getting Manuelo to impersonate a famous movie director and then calling up Tedi. The rest of her plan had something to do with asking Tedi to be in a movie about modeling, but it was so silly that Chloe couldn't even follow it.

Tara's best idea was to just lie to Tedi and tell her the job paid a quarter of a million dollars.

"No. It has to be something better," Quinn insisted.

"Yeah," Chloe agreed. "She'd never fall for that. I just wish we could show her how good she has it. Being a model is an awesome job."

"I've got it!" Quinn cried. "How about a dose of real life? The *opposite* of a fan club."

"Hmm," Amanda said. "This sounds good."

"What if you go to the mall with Tedi," Quinn went on, "and then we show up and *accidentally* run into you guys. But we don't recognize Tedi or anything. We just ignore her. You said she was bummed about not being mobbed this morning. Maybe if it keeps happening to her, she'll start to miss being famous."

Chloe wasn't sure. It *might* work. Then again it might not. Tedi was pretty determined to be ordinary.

But what other choice did Chloe have?

At least it was worth a try.

chapter
six

"**W**ho is that?" Chloe whispered to Manuelo.

She had just walked into the kitchen after school on Monday. Someone new—a very beautiful model—was standing in the living room, modeling one of Macy's dresses.

Before Manuelo could answer, the whole house rattled with the sound of breaking glass.

Crash!

Chloe jumped. She and Manuelo ran to see what had happened. A broken vase was lying on the living room floor.

"Oh, I'm so sorry!" the model said, backing away. "I didn't see it there."

"Oh, Manuelo!" Chloe whispered. She covered her mouth, horrified. "Is that the vase your mother gave you, that you gave us?"

Manuelo nodded, scowling.

"Who is she?" Chloe whispered again.

"Your mother is trying *desperately* to find a lead model," Manuelo explained. "But no one is available. Except *her*." He spit the last word.

"But who *is* she?" Chloe asked for the third time.

"Elissa Natalia," Manuelo said.

Chloe gasped when she heard the name.

Elissa Natalia? She was a model who was famous for being horribly clumsy. She always tripped, fell, or spilled things on the clothes. Or all three. Macy had used Elissa once five years ago. But never again.

"She's a walking time bomb," Manuelo said.

"Shh!" Chloe scolded him. "She'll hear you."

"I don't care!" Manuelo said. "Look at what she did already!" He pointed at the pile of broken glass in the living room.

Then Chloe saw her mother standing there, covering her eyes with her hands.

Macy shook her head, as if she didn't know what to say. She handed Elissa another dress to try on.

"I'll be right back," Elissa said, heading across the living room toward the hall bathroom. But on the way, her foot caught on a different dress draped across the couch. She tripped, falling forward. The hem of the dress she was wearing caught on the corner of the coffee table and tore. "Oh, sorry!" she said, dashing out of the room.

Macy threw up her hands and stormed into the kitchen.

44

From the scarlet color of her mom's face, Chloe could tell she was almost hysterical.

"What am I going to do?" Macy cried.

"Don't worry, Mom," Chloe whispered. "She's really beautiful. So she's a little clumsy. Still, your clothes will look great on her. It could work out."

Macy whisper-screamed, "But she's already ruined three dresses!"

"Three?" Chloe was surprised.

"I forgot to tell you," Manuelo said. "She got lipstick on the neckline of the first thing she tried on."

Chloe winced. Getting lipstick on a dress was a major crime in their house. Worse than failing a test or forgetting to walk the dog.

"Isn't there anyone else you could hire?" Chloe asked her mom.

Macy shook her head. "I guess we'll have to stick with Elissa," she said miserably.

Not if I have anything to say about it, Chloe thought.

This was serious. Way serious.

"Can you believe those waves?" Alex stared out the window at California Dream and then at Riley. "Makes me wish I surfed."

"Oh, I can just see you on a surfboard—with your guitar in your hands," Riley teased him. "I mean, how would you ever manage to stand up?"

45

"Hey, I put my guitar down sometimes," Alex protested, shooting her a cute smile. "Like now, for instance."

True, Riley thought. He was supposed to be rehearsing with The Wave. But he had moved the rehearsal time so he could spend the afternoon with her first.

"Maybe you guys should change the band's name to Electric Wave," she joked.

"How about Shock Wave?" Alex shot back.

Riley laughed and glanced toward the door. Someone had just walked in. Someone with long wavy blond hair like Chloe's. For a minute, Riley thought it was her sister. But it wasn't.

"What's wrong?" Alex reached across the table and took Riley's hand.

"It's Chloe," Riley answered, wishing that Chloe *had* walked in. "She's been totally weird lately, like she doesn't care about anyone but herself."

"Whoa. What's up? What did she do?" Alex asked.

"Lots of stuff," Riley said. "I told you how she borrowed my new top on Friday without asking, right?"

Alex nodded.

"Well, then she did it again on Saturday. The same blouse! I think she took some eyeliner, too."

Alex shrugged. "Is that a major crime? Because it doesn't sound so bad."

"It's bad, believe me," Riley said. But she had to

admit that now that she was saying it aloud, it seemed to have lost some of its impact. "Then there's the whole Larry-debate-partner mess," she added, "which is Chloe's fault, too."

"He's still acting weirder than weird when he tries to speak?" Alex asked, taking a swig of his vanilla malt.

"He can't help it," Riley said, nodding. "I thought I had him cured of the giggles until we practiced in front of Manuelo."

"Well, if anyone can cure him, you can," Alex said.

"Thanks." Riley sipped her latte and stared into Alex's dark brown eyes. He was so awesome. And he looked so cute with his sandy brown hair falling over his forehead.

"But I don't see how the Larry thing is Chloe's fault," Alex added.

"It is. I wouldn't even *be* in the debate club if she hadn't asked me to join with her," Riley explained. "And then she stuck me with Larry as a partner. And *then* she forgot to give me your phone message, remember?"

"Yeah, that's not cool," Alex agreed, nodding sympathetically. "But you know—"

"Uh-oh." Riley clapped a hand over her mouth. "I just remembered something."

"What?"

"I forgot to give *her* a phone message. Eric called Saturday night when she was at Tara's house," Riley admitted. "And I forgot to tell her to call him back."

"Forgot on purpose?" Alex asked.

"No way! It was just a mistake," Riley insisted.

"So maybe she just forgot your message the same way?" Alex asked.

"I don't know...." Riley admitted. Her voice trailed off. "It just seems as if Chloe isn't thinking a *bit* about my feelings these days. She's so clueless, I'll bet she doesn't even know I'm mad at her. She probably doesn't even know what a jerk she's being!"

"Uh, earth to Riley," Alex said. "If she doesn't know, then how can she make things better? I mean, you've got to tell her how you feel. How can you guys work it out if you're the only person who knows you're mad?"

"I'm not the only one," Riley argued. "Sierra knows."

Alex tilted his head and smiled. "Come on. That's totally lame."

"Yeah," Riley said. "I guess I should talk to Chloe."

"Definitely," Alex said. "I mean, don't let this become a real fight—not with Chloe. Not over dumb stuff like phone messages."

Yeah, Riley thought. That's what Sierra said, too.

"Okay, okay," Riley promised. She felt much better already. "I'll talk to Chloe as soon as I get home tonight."

chapter
seven

Chloe stared down from the second floor at the fountain on the main level of the mall. She and her friends were watching and waiting for Tedi to arrive.

"Where is she?" Amanda asked.

"She said she'd meet me in front of the fountain at five o'clock," Chloe explained.

"Well, she's late," Amanda said. "Not that I mind hanging out in the mall all day—don't get me wrong. But I've got a huge paper to write for English."

"Hey, chill," Tara said to Amanda. "We're here on a mission to save Chloe's mom from professional disaster! How often do you get to shop and feel like you're doing something good for humanity at the same time?"

"Oh, right," Quinn joked. "I can see your bumper sticker now: 'I shop to save the planet.'"

"Maybe she's not coming," Amanda worried. "What if this whole plan doesn't work?"

Don't say that, Chloe thought. It's got to work. Because if it doesn't...

"There she is!" Quinn nudged Chloe and pointed.

Chloe followed Quinn's finger and saw Tedi standing on the far side of the fountain.

Weird, Chloe thought. I almost didn't recognize her in those jeans and that plain white T-shirt!

From the looks of it, Tedi was dressing down again, trying to look like a regular person.

"Okay, just keep your eyes on us," Chloe instructed her friends. "Tedi and I will head down toward the main mall entrance. You can follow us from up here and then come down the far escalator and run into us. Got it?"

"Ten-four," Tara joked, saluting.

Chloe hurried down the back escalator and rushed up to Tedi as if she'd just arrived at the mall.

"Hey, girlfriend," Tedi said, smiling. "So what's up? Two shopping trips in three days? Not that I'm complaining. I'm totally loving it."

Loving it? That's not what I want to hear! Chloe thought.

"So what's the emergency?" Tedi asked.

"Well, I need some shoes to go with these new hot pink pants I bought," Chloe said. She pulled the skinny pants out of her bag. "See?"

"They're wild," Tedi said. "Very retro, huh?"

"Right," Chloe said. "But I can't decide what kind of shoes to buy. Do I go for the retro spiked heels to go with the pants, or will that just make me look like a tramp?"

"Before I answer, tell me this: Do you *want* to look like a tramp?" Tedi asked.

"No!" Chloe blurted out. "I mean, I'm not the trashy type."

"That's what I thought," Tedi said, "but I was just checking."

"So?" Chloe waited for her advice.

"So I'd say go for something fun instead," Tedi advised. "Maybe some crazy canvas shoes in, like, a totally cool print—for contrast."

"I knew you'd have a great idea, Tedi!" Chloe said honestly.

Chloe had already started walking through the mall. She was tempted to look up, to see if her friends were following from above, but she didn't dare.

"Are you thinking what I'm thinking?" Tedi asked.

I doubt it, Chloe thought. I'm thinking about the major plot my friends and I are trying to pull to manipulate you into going back to modeling.

Chloe raised her eyebrows.

"B&B Shoes?" Tedi said.

"Exactly!" Chloe agreed.

"That's what I thought," Tedi said. "They're having an incredible sale."

[**Chloe**: Okay, I hate to sound like a whiner, but this hanging out with Tedi thing is starting to cost me. Big-time. I've already shelled out more

than I was planning to spend on Saturday. Now
I'm probably going to end up with another pair of
shoes. All I can say is: The sacrifices I make for
my mom are worth it.]

When they were a few stores away from B&B Shoes,
Chloe saw Amanda, Tara, and Quinn coming down the
escalator in front of them. But she pretended not to
notice.

Let them come up to me, she thought. It's better
that way.

"Chlo-eeee!"

It was Tara's voice. She was laying it on thick—the
fake surprise.

"Tara, hi-eeee!" Chloe said, doing the same thing,
acting totally amazed to run into them.

Quinn and Amanda were just a little bit behind
Tara. Chloe could see they were deliberately not making
eye contact with Tedi.

In fact, they're almost being rude, Chloe thought, by
ignoring Tedi completely. I can't just treat her as if she
isn't even here, she realized. That would be bad manners.

"What are you doing?" Quinn asked Chloe, barely
glancing at Tedi.

"Shoe shopping," Chloe answered. "To go with
those new pants I bought."

Quinn nodded.

"Um, this is Tedi," Chloe said, pretending to intro-
duce them. "She used to model for my mom."

"Really?" Quinn put a look on her face that said, *Are you kidding me?*

That's so mean! Chloe thought. But she had to admit it was clever. Still, she didn't feel good about treating Tedi this way.

Tedi sort of blinked, but Chloe couldn't tell if the treatment was getting to her or not.

"Oh, hi," Tara said to Tedi, also looking really surprised. "I didn't recognize you."

"So anyway," Amanda said, jumping in really quick, as if she couldn't care less about meeting Tedi, "we've got to go. We're on a mission to find a birthday present for my dad."

"See you tomorrow," Chloe called as they moved off down the mall. That was stupid, she thought when it was all over. Then she cleared her throat and looked at Tedi. "Wow! That was way weird. I totally thought they'd recognize you!"

"Hey, that's good with me," Tedi said with a shrug.

"Really?" Chloe asked.

"Definitely!" Tedi said. "It's so much easier to hang out when people aren't swarming all over you. I'm having the best time just being normal like everyone else. Honestly, I haven't had this much fun in months!"

Fun? How am I going to get her to go back to modeling if she's having a good time being a regular person?

"So let's buy some shoes!" Tedi said, marching off toward B&B.

Chloe tried, but she just couldn't get into shopping. She wasn't in the mood. Nothing interested her. *I wish Riley were here,* she thought.

Or at least she wished she could talk to Riley when she got home. Maybe this whole thing with Tedi was too much for her to handle on her own. After all, her plan wasn't exactly working. At this rate, her mom's show on Friday was going to be awful.

"Well, do you want to give up?" Tedi said.

"Huh?" Chloe felt a little panicky. *Did Tedi know about her plan all along?*

"On the shoes," Tedi said. "Hey, earth to Chloe. You look like you're just not into this today."

"Oh. Yeah," Chloe said. She glanced at the pile of shoes at her feet. She'd tried on four pairs, and she had to admit that they were *all* really cute and would look amazing with her pants. "Yeah, I guess you're right."

Tedi swung her tote bag over her shoulder and strolled through the mall toward the exit.

She looks so happy, Chloe thought as they walked, which made her feel even more miserable about this whole thing.

"I just love being average," Tedi said. "Isn't this a hoot?"

That's just because she doesn't know what an average *person does every day,* Chloe realized.

All Tedi had done since she'd quit modeling was shop! Who wouldn't *be happy with that?*

If only there was some way to show Tedi what the real world was like. And Chloe didn't mean a behind-the-scenes tour at MTV!

Chloe gazed around the crowded mall. She spotted two kids in red and white Pizza Paradise uniforms, heading into the fast-food joint.

Then her eye landed on a sign in the window next door: HELP WANTED. START IMMEDIATELY!

That's it! If Tedi had to work a regular boring day job, she'd realize how lucky she was to be a model!

And this job looked perfect, too. It was a photography portrait studio. The kind of place where moms brought their drooling, screaming one-year-olds to have their pictures taken in front of some kind of cheesy background. It was super-tough, even for the most patient person in the world.

"Hey, look," Chloe said, pointing to the HELP WANTED sign. "If you really want to be average, why don't you apply for that job?"

Tedi slowed down, read the sign, and paused. She shot Chloe an interested glance. "Do you think?" she said.

"Oh, yeah," Chloe said, selling the idea like crazy. "I mean, it could be a *hoot* being behind the camera for a change. And you're already a natural for this job. You know all kinds of stuff about lighting and posing."

"Yeah!" Tedi was really getting into it.

"Go on," Chloe urged her. "Why don't you apply right now? I'll just hang back."

And if you don't get hired, even better! Chloe thought. That would be a dose of reality!

"Hey, why not? I don't have anything better to do!" Tedi agreed.

That's what you think! Chloe thought.

She watched while Tedi talked to the studio's manager. The minute Tedi caught his eye, she started turning on the charm. It was amazing. Even in blue jeans and a T-shirt, she suddenly looked glamorous.

That's why she gets the big bucks modeling, Chloe realized. She knows how to light up from the inside.

A few minutes later Tedi had the job.

"He needs me to start right now," Tedi explained quickly. "Do you mind?"

"No problem," Chloe said. "I'll just hang out for a while and watch."

Chloe stepped back and watched while the manager showed Tedi how to work the camera equipment.

Then some customers came in. The first was a young mother with a two-year-old daughter. The little girl kept begging for a cookie, but her mom wouldn't give it to her. She didn't want her daughter to mess up her dress.

Excellent, Chloe thought. Cranky and hungry kid. Stressed-out mom. Recipe for disaster.

But Tedi charmed the little girl instantly. "Hi," she said, bending down. "I *love* your dress!"

The little girl started to grin.

"You want to have your picture taken in that pretty, pretty dress?" Tedi asked in a really sweet voice.

The little girl nodded and hopped up on the posing stand in front of the camera.

Tedi beamed and shot Chloe a pleased-as-punch smile.

Oh, perfect, Chloe thought, frowning. Who knew Tedi was so fabulous with kids? She's a regular Mary Poppins!

Chloe turned quietly and slipped out of the store. All my ideas are backfiring, she thought. Instead of making Tedi feel sorry she's not a model, I got her a new job. And she loves it!

Was there anything else that could possibly go wrong?

chapter
eight

"**I** need a Perrier with lemon right away," a tall, beautiful model with wavy black hair told Riley. The woman was surrounded by a bunch of people dressed in black.

"Excuse me?" Riley's eyes popped wide open.

She had just walked into the house from her date with Alex and found the living room packed with people.

"Hurry up!" the model snapped. "I'm parched here."

Whoa! Riley thought. Who does she think she is, giving me orders that way?

In fact, who *is* she, anyway?

Riley gazed around at the crowd. First there was the model—someone she'd never seen before. She was glaring at Riley right now as if Riley were some kind of pond scum.

Then there were all of the model's friends and assistants—people just hanging out, doing nothing. One was obviously a hairdresser. Another was a makeup person. The rest of them were reading fashion magazines and drinking diet colas.

Riley hurried into the kitchen and cornered Manuelo. "Who is that person?" she asked him.

"That's number three. You missed numbers one and two," Manuelo said.

"Huh?"

"Your mother is auditioning more models today," Manuelo explained.

"Why?" Riley wondered. "What happened to Tedi?"

"She quit," Manuelo declared.

"What?" Riley's mouth fell open in shock.

"Last week," Manuelo reported. "On Friday. And now your poor mother is stranded with no one to model her designs in four days. Didn't you know? I thought Chloe told you."

"Are you kidding me?" Riley said, still stunned.

Manuelo nodded. "It's horrible," he said. "I thought you knew about it, but I guess you haven't been around much lately."

Wow, Riley thought. I guess I *have* been wrapped up in my own problems for the past couple of days.

She looked through the open door at the model in the living room and then at her mother. Macy was in total panic mode.

This is big, Riley realized. Really big. Not like all the other crises her mom was used to. From the look on her mom's face, Riley could tell she was seriously worried.

And with good reason.

"Is Chloe home?" Riley asked Manuelo.

He nodded. "She just got here," he said. "She's upstairs."

Why didn't she tell me about this? Riley wondered. How come I'm the last to hear about it? Great. Now Mom probably thinks I don't care about her problems. Thanks a lot, Chloe!

Riley felt her face starting to get hot, but then she took a deep breath. Calm down, she told herself. Don't let this stuff get blown out of proportion.

Talk to Chloe.

That's what Alex said, right? And Sierra?

Riley got a bottle of Perrier for the model. Then she started up the stairs to her room. But halfway up she stopped.

"Are you kidding?" the model was saying in a really nasty voice. "You want me to wear *that*?"

"Well, I'm still working on the length," Macy admitted, holding up an ice-blue silk gown she had designed. "But yes, I'm going to pair it with flat silver shoes and a gauzy shawl."

The model laughed and shot a glance at one of her friends. "You want me to wear *flat* shoes," she said, her voice filled with disgust.

Riley hurried back to the kitchen. "She's evil!" she whispered to Manuelo. "How can Mom use her?"

"She has no choice," Manuelo said. "She needs a headliner for her fashion show and all the good models are already booked."

"All of them?" Riley was surprised.

"This one is the worst so far, though," Manuelo whispered. "First she brings her entire entourage. Then she told your mother she won't do the show unless she can use her own makeup guy and pick the music for the runway herself!"

"That's outrageous!" Riley said. "It's Mom's show!"

"I know," Manuelo said, shaking his head. "And she's no prize. She got fired from her last job for showing up late. Then she told the designer he was lucky she showed up at all!" He sighed. "I miss Tedi."

Riley closed her eyes. This was an emergency! She and Chloe should do something to help Mom.

But first she needed to talk to Chloe about the other stuff. She ran up the stairs and burst into their bedroom.

Chloe was sprawled on her bed. She looked like she was in a rotten mood herself.

"Hi," Riley said, trying to get to the point quickly. "Listen, I'm ready to forgive you."

"Forgive me?" Chloe's eyes opened wide. "Are you kidding? Forgive me for what?"

"For all the stuff you've been doing," Riley said. "I mean, you borrowed my new top and you forgot my phone message from Alex. But I guess that's really little stuff compared with what Mom is going through downstairs."

"Look, if you're going to blame me for Mom's problems..." Chloe snapped.

Blame her for Mom's problems? No way, Riley thought. What did Chloe have to do with that?

"I'm not blaming you," Riley said. "I told you, I'm ready to forgive you! I mean, you did all this stuff and then you forgot to give me Alex's message—"

"Oh, nice. First you try to make me feel guilty and then you forgive me! Thanks a lot!" Chloe shouted.

"Whoa. Calm down," Riley said.

"Why should I calm down?" Chloe snapped. "I'm not the only one who forgets phone messages around here! What about my phone call from Eric that *someone* never bothered to mention to me? He's totally mad because I didn't call him back on Saturday. And *who* was the one who didn't give me that message? You!"

"Look, what I'm trying to say is, we shouldn't be fighting about phone messages," Riley said. "It's stupid."

Chloe's eyes flashed with anger. "Are you calling me *stupid*?"

"No, I—" Riley tried to say.

"Don't even talk to me!" Chloe said. "I'm too angry with you." Then she got up, turned her back, and walked over to her desk as if the conversation were closed.

Unbelievable! Riley thought. I try to talk to her—and forgive her—and she gives me the cold shoulder. And after all the things Chloe has done to me!

Riley was fuming inside, but she wasn't going to

storm out of the room. No way. She didn't want to give Chloe the satisfaction. Instead, she sat down at her desk in the opposite corner and opened a book.

Concentrate, she told herself as she tried to read over her notes for the big debate. It was only three days away and she and Larry hadn't really nailed it yet.

But she couldn't focus. Chloe was tapping her pencil on the desk in a really annoying way. She's doing it to get on my nerves, Riley thought.

Chloe flipped on her computer and logged on-line.

"You've got mail!" the computer chimed.

Riley sighed loudly. Can't she turn off those sounds? Doesn't she realize I'm trying to study?

Her sister was searching through a Web site, and every time she clicked her mouse, the computer made a beeping noise.

She's definitely doing it on purpose, Riley thought.

Fine! If she wants to fight, two can play at that game. Riley started humming a song from kindergarten that Chloe had always despised. "Hmm, hmmm-hmm, hmmmmmm, hm-hm-hm-hm hmmm-hm-hm."

Chloe tapped her pencil louder. And faster.

"Could you be quiet?" Riley said. "I'm trying to study for the debate."

"Why bother?" Chloe snapped. "With Larry as a partner, you aren't going to win, anyway."

"That's what you think," Riley shot back. "Larry will be great. You'll see!"

"Whatever." Chloe dropped her pencil hard on the desk.

No, I think she threw it, Riley realized.

Okay, that's it, she decided. I've had it. If it's war Chloe wants, it's war she's going to get!

chapter
nine

"**P**lease pass the strawberry jam," Riley said to Chloe the next morning in that cool, polite, I'm-not-really-speaking-to-you tone of hers.

Chloe winced, but she tried not to let it show. Go ahead, Riley, she thought. Act like nothing's wrong in front of Mom.

She sent the small glass dish of strawberry preserves over to her sister without making eye contact.

"So," Manuelo said, trying to make conversation. "What are my two favorite Malibu teenagers up to for the rest of this week?"

"Nothing," Riley said.

"Nothing." Chloe used the same dull tone of voice Riley did.

"Nothing?" Manuelo tried to sound cheery. "But aren't you both in a debate with Larry the Laugher?"

"Uh-huh." Riley stared down at her food.

Chloe didn't say anything. There was another awkward silence.

"Is your bagel toasted enough?" Manuelo asked Chloe.

"Uh-huh," Chloe replied.

He shook his head. "You two must not be getting enough sleep," he said. "Because you both sound like you're only half alive this morning."

I'm alive, Chloe thought. I just don't want to make conversation with someone who hates me!

[Chloe: Not that I blame her. I kind of flipped out yesterday. But I promise you that's not really me. To tell the truth, I wasn't even angry with Riley. I was mad at myself for ruining Mom's show by talking Tedi into quitting. I haven't been that loony since the time I overslept and missed the 3-for-1 bathing suit sale at Saks. Can you imagine how crazy that would make YOU? But, of course, the Tedi thing is a much bigger deal. Somehow I'm going to have to find a way to tell Mom that it was all my fault. And then I'll apologize to Riley. Somehow.]

"Manuelo! Chloe! Riley! Good news!" Macy called, hurrying into the kitchen. "I've found someone!"

Chloe's head shot up. "You have? A model?"

Macy nodded.

"That's fabulous, Mom!" Chloe said. "Who?"

Macy held up a finger. She glanced toward the hall bathroom and raised her eyebrows. "Ready?" she called to someone who was standing out of sight.

While Macy stood there beaming, a beautiful young model swept into the kitchen wearing Macy's most elegant design. It was the long, cream-colored silk dress—the one Elissa had gotten lipstick on. But the lipstick was gone.

"Meet Bernadette," Macy said, introducing her to everyone. "Bernadette, these are my daughters—Chloe and Riley. And you already know Manuelo."

"Hi," Bernadette said. She did a little twirl to show off the dress.

"Ooh," Manuelo said, covering his mouth and gushing over the model. "She's a vision!"

She looks perfect! Chloe thought, happy for the first time in days. She's graceful and beautiful. Maybe even prettier than Tedi! I wonder why I've never seen her before.

Bernadette was carrying a bouquet of creamy white daisies tied up with satin ribbon. Her hair was pinned up in a beautiful series of French braids and twists.

"Wow," Riley said. "Mom, she looks awesome!"

"Is that a wedding dress?" Chloe asked.

Macy shook her head. "It's not *the* wedding dress. I have another one—a traditional gown. But I'm showing this with flowers so that if someone wants a simpler wedding option..."

Just then, Bernadette sneezed. It came on so unexpected, she tossed the flowers onto the floor so she could use both hands to cover her nose. "Excuse me!"

"Bless you," Manuelo said quickly.

"Sorry," Bernadette said, picking up the flowers. But an instant later she sneezed again. "Ahh-choo!"

She dropped the flowers again and grabbed for some tissues. "Oh, gosh, sorry," Bernadette said. "I seem to be allergic to something."

Before Chloe could hand her the box of tissues, she started sneezing again. And this time she didn't stop. She sneezed over and over, grabbing for tissues. Pretty soon her eyes were watering so much that mascara was running down her face.

"I don't know what's going—ahhh-chooo!" she said. "Excuse me!"

"Bless you," Manuelo said, although this time he sounded more frustrated than kind.

Chloe caught a glimpse of the panicked look in her mom's eyes.

"Bernadette," Macy said, "are you allergic to daisies?"

"I must be," she said. "I'm allergic to tons of things."

Macy rolled her eyes.

I know exactly what she's thinking, Chloe realized. So *that's* why this girl hasn't done much modeling!

Bernadette sneezed again and ran out of the room. "Excuse me, I'd better take off this dress," she said.

"What are you going to do, Mom?" Chloe asked.

"What *can* I do?" Macy said. "I've got to use her.

There's no other choice." She bit her fingernail and stared down the hall toward the bathroom. Bernadette was in there, still sneezing. "I guess I won't use real flowers," Macy said sadly.

Maybe there *was* another choice, Chloe thought. Maybe if Chloe and her friends went to the mall, they'd see that Tedi hated her new job. And then they'd be able to talk her into modeling again. That was possible, wasn't it?

Maybe.

"So you tried to talk to her and she yelled at you?" Sierra asked Riley. It was after school, and the two girls were getting ready to leave.

Riley pulled three books out of her locker and slammed it shut. "Yes. I tried to be reasonable, but she acted as if I was the one to blame. We had a majorly huge argument."

Sierra shook her head. "I don't get it. You and Chloe hardly ever fight. I mean, what's up with her?"

"I don't know," Riley said, exasperated. "And right now I don't care, either. I've got other things to think about."

Sierra twisted a clump of her red hair into a knot and flipped a rubber band around it. "You mean Larry?" she guessed.

Riley nodded.

Sierra tossed her backpack over her shoulder and headed for the door. "Well, look," she said. "If worse comes to worst, and he's still giggling like a hyena at the debate on Thursday, I'll put Plan B into action."

"What's Plan B?" Riley asked. "I didn't know we had a Plan B."

"I'll get a group of people to chant his name every time he starts to speak," Sierra explained. She pumped a fist in the air. "Lar-ry! Lar-ry! Lar-ry! It'll drown out the sound of him laughing onstage."

Riley smiled. Sierra wasn't serious, but it definitely helped. "Thanks," she said as they split up to head home.

"No problem," Sierra called. "You know I've got your back."

Riley sort of wanted to stop at home and drop off her backpack. But she didn't want to run into Chloe. So she went straight to Larry's house.

When he opened the door, she smelled popcorn. Then she saw the dining table. It was spread with all kinds of snacks and treats. There was a big tray of strawberries with powdered sugar, some nachos, a plate of brownies, a bowl of popcorn, some gummy candies, and a bottle of sparkling apple cider.

Josh Edelman and Ben O'Connor, two of Larry's friends, were sitting in the living room. Riley said hi to them both.

"Hi," Josh said, nodding toward Riley. He was a really small guy who wore thick Buddy Holly glasses.

Ben was kind of chubby. He was lying on the couch reading a comic book and didn't look up.

"Larry, what is this?" Riley asked, pointing to the table. "We're supposed to be practicing for the debate, not partying like there's no tomorrow."

"It's my new system," Larry said. "I give myself a treat each time I score a good point in the debate. I've been practicing for half an hour, and I've eaten most of the nachos. Sorry."

Riley rolled her eyes. This could take a while, she thought. And get messy. There were already some blobs of nacho cheese on the floor.

But if his new system was working...if it kept Larry from laughing, she was willing to give it a try.

"So you aren't getting nervous in front of Josh and Ben?" Riley asked.

"I don't know," Larry said. "They just got here."

"Okay." She nodded. "Let's see what happens now that you have an audience. Are you ready to get to work?"

"Sure, but do you want some champagne first?" Larry asked. He held up a bottle.

"That's not champagne. It's apple cider," Riley corrected him. "And actually I'd love some. I'm really thirsty. But then we've got to get busy. The debate is only two days away!"

Riley drank her cider and then stood up in the middle of the room. "I'll go first," she said. "That way, I can get us into a serious mood."

At least she hoped so. She was desperate to cure

Larry of his nervousness and beat Chloe in the debate. After the way Chloe had been treating her, she deserved to lose in front of the whole school!

Riley cleared her throat and started out with all of her arguments about how homeless people couldn't help being homeless.

Josh and Ben stared at her, totally bored. But she didn't care. She stepped aside to let Larry take over.

"When do we get to eat?" Ben asked.

"Not yet," Riley said. "Just listen."

Larry stood up and cleared his throat. "Everything my partner, Riley, said is true," Larry began.

But almost immediately he started to giggle.

"She's right. Homeless people have...have...rights... ha-ha-ha-ha!"

"Larry!" Riley cried.

"I know, I know," Larry said, still snickering. "I just can't help it."

"Okay, that's it," Riley said. "Josh, Ben, you guys have to go. We aren't getting anywhere with you here."

"Can I take the gummy candy?" Josh asked.

"Whatever." Riley waved them away.

When they were gone, she sat Larry down on the couch for a heart-to-heart talk.

"Listen, we've got to figure this out," Riley said. "What's making you so nervous?"

"I don't know," Larry said. "Honestly, I didn't feel nervous at all. I really think I'm over that."

"Then why are you laughing?" Riley asked. "What were you thinking about when you were standing up there debating in front of Josh and Ben?"

"Underwear," Larry admitted.

"Huh?" Riley's mouth dropped open. That was the last thing she'd expected to hear.

"Underwear," Larry repeated. "My cousin Becky gave me this trick to get over being nervous in front of a group. She said I should just imagine the whole audience sitting in their underwear."

[Riley: Okay, from now on I'm wearing a trench coat in front of Larry.]

"Well, that's your problem right there," Riley said.

"Probably," Larry admitted. "I mean, I know for a fact that Josh still wears this old pair of Superman Underoos. It's hysterical!"

Riley rolled her eyes. "Of course you're going to laugh if you start thinking about stuff like that," she said. "Does he really wear Superman underwear?" It was hard to believe.

Larry nodded. "And Spider-Man."

Riley tried not to crack a smile. "Well, that's beside the point. We've got to come up with something else for you to think about. Something *not* funny."

"Like plain underwear?" Larry suggested.

Riley sighed. "It's a start."

chapter
ten

"**A**re you kidding?" Eric said on Wednesday after school. "The debate is tomorrow!"

"I know, I know. I'm really sorry," Chloe said. "But I can't practice today. There's a major family crisis I've got to take care of. Can we do it tomorrow morning maybe? Before school?"

Eric squinted at her as if he thought she was nuts. "Look, we've got to work on this," he said. "You can't just stand up in front of the whole school and wing it."

"In front of the whole school?" Chloe gulped. Wow. She hadn't thought about that part. This was a chance for utter humiliation. "I mean, how many people come to these debates?" she asked.

"It's held in the auditorium and the place is usually packed." Eric gave her a *What-did-you-think*? glare. "West Malibu rocks at debate. We usually go to the Nationals, so everyone shows up to support us."

"Wow. Okay, okay, we need to practice," Chloe agreed. "But I can't today. There's an emergency—something I've got to do for my mom."

"Well, I can't get an early ride to school tomorrow," Eric said.

"How about working on it during study hall?" Chloe suggested.

Eric shook his head. "That's not going to be enough."

Just then Tara and Quinn hurried up to her. "Are we going to the mall or what?" Tara asked. "We're waiting for you."

Eric glared at Chloe, and she could see what he was thinking. The mall? That was the family emergency? That was what was more important than practicing for the debate?

He shook his head again and walked off, leaving her standing by her locker.

Chloe swallowed hard. She felt awful blowing off the debate practice. But she couldn't help it. The thing with Tedi was more important. "Yeah, I'm ready," she said.

"Is Amanda coming?" Tara asked.

"She's meeting us there," Chloe explained.

The mall was crowded with people checking out some big Wednesday sale at the department store near where Tedi worked. Chloe and her friends met Amanda by the fountain, then hurried to see how Tedi was doing.

"I should be getting my mail delivered here," Chloe joked. "I've been here three times in five days."

"Is that more than usual?" Quinn asked.

"Sounds like you're slacking off to me," Tara said. "A really devoted shopper wouldn't skip so often."

Amanda smiled but didn't say anything.

They hurried through the mall to the photography studio.

"Hey, look," Tara said as they approached. "The place is packed."

"Good," Chloe said.

"Check it out. Tedi totally has her hands full," Quinn said.

No kidding! Chloe thought. Tedi was holding twin babies—one rested on her hip and the other one she gripped under her arm like a football. She looked like she was going to drop one of them at any minute.

The four girls got as close as they could without being seen by Tedi.

The twins' mother, a nervous-looking young woman with stringy brown hair, ran up to Tedi and took one of the babies from her. She put the infant on the posing stand and started changing his diaper.

Amanda giggled.

"What's so funny?" Chloe asked.

"I was just thinking, it's a long way from modeling string bikinis to changing diapers," Amanda replied. "Tedi's totally getting a taste of real life."

Just then, the other baby puked on Tedi's silk shirt.

Tara and Quinn laughed, and Chloe couldn't help giggling, too.

"You guys are so terrible," Amanda whispered, although there was a definite smile on her mouth.

"We're not terrible," Chloe protested. "I'm just glad to see Tedi having a bad time. If she doesn't quit this job and start modeling again by Friday, my mom's show will flop. And then Mom will be looking for a job at the mall!"

Chloe watched from behind a pillar for a few more minutes. Tedi was trying hard, but the mothers were getting restless.

One woman started complaining that they'd been waiting an hour. Then, just as Tedi was ready to take a picture of the twins, another kid ran up and knocked over the lights.

Tedi heaved a huge sigh and looked as if she wanted to strangle the boy.

"She's freaking out," Quinn said.

"Yeah, but she's not ready to quit on the spot," Amanda pointed out.

"Right," Chloe said. "So what should I do? Go up to her and just tell her the truth? That Mom needs her to come back?"

"Not yet," Tara said. "Give her a few more days to get really sick of this."

"I don't have a few more days!" Chloe said. "This is Wednesday! My mom's show is Friday!"

"I have an idea," Amanda said quietly. "I've been doing some baby-sitting for a really bratty kid."

Chloe's eyes lit up. She liked the sound of this.

"Tell me about it," Quinn said. "I sit for two total monsters."

Amanda nodded. "Yeah. I'll bet we all know some real terrors if we think about it. So what if we all bring in the brattiest kids we can find and have their pictures taken here? By the time we're done, Tedi will want to quit for sure!"

"That's brilliant!" Chloe said. Then her face fell. "But there's no time left. I've got to do this debate thing tomorrow after school."

Amanda shrugged. "The mall is open till nine and the photo studio is, too. We'll come after the debate. I'll bet if we tell the moms we're taking their kids off their hands for free, they'll want to adopt us!"

"You're the best!" Chloe said, hugging Amanda.

"Hey, what about me?" Tara said. "I know some annoying kids. Don't I get a hug?"

Chloe laughed and hugged all of them. Her friends were awesome!

But in the back of her mind she couldn't help worrying. What if this plan didn't work? Then there would be nothing else she could do. She was totally out of time and ideas.

This was her very last chance.

chapter
eleven

"Riley, what's wrong?" Larry whispered from the back of the school auditorium.

On the stage in front of her, Riley watched the other debate teams. The sophomores and juniors were onstage. They were getting up, one by one, and making their points.

But Riley could barely listen. Her face was set in a tight frown.

"What is it?" Larry asked again.

What's wrong? Riley thought. Nothing. Nothing except that my sister likes to start fights when she's the one who's wrong.

"I'm just nervous," Riley answered truthfully. "I really want to win."

"Don't worry. We will," Larry said confidently.

Riley shot him a glance. "Really?"

She hoped he was right, because she'd been waiting

for this debate ever since her big fight with Chloe. Ever since Chloe was so horrible and wouldn't let Riley forgive her.

And then Chloe had the nerve to say that Riley and Larry didn't stand a chance of winning the debate.

Riley had been so totally furious that all she could think about was beating Chloe and teaching her a thing or two.

"Don't worry," Larry repeated in a whisper, trying to reassure her. "I'm fine. I won't laugh. I promise."

He's said that before, Riley thought. But what if he does laugh—in front of the whole school? What if we lose the debate? What if Chloe turns out to be right?

The longer she stood there, the more upset she got. This was going to be a disaster, she suddenly realized. A horrible, embarrassing, humiliating disaster.

Larry would make them both look like fools in front of the whole school. And then Chloe would win and Riley would never hear the end of it.

"Come on," Larry whispered. "We're on next."

Larry led her by the sleeve to the backstage area, where all the debate teams were supposed to wait.

Where is she? Riley wondered, looking around. Chloe and Eric should be backstage now, too. They were supposed to go on right after Riley and Larry.

As soon as the sophomore debaters finished, it was Riley's turn. She and Larry walked to the middle of the stage.

Riley sat on a folding chair beside the podium. Larry stood up, cleared his throat, and began.

"There are so many reasons why we, as a society, should be tolerant and understanding enough to allow homeless people to sleep in public places," Larry said, coolly and calmly.

Wow, Riley thought, sitting up. He's doing it. He sounds great!

"For one thing, homeless people have already suffered the indignity of not having a home," Larry argued. "Why should we make their burden so much worse by making them feel bad about it? Can't we, as the richest country on earth, afford to have a little compassion? Instead of working to get these people off the streets, why aren't we working to find them places to sleep?"

Riley was impressed. He sounded calm and thoughtful, his voice wasn't cracking or stammering, and he had planned out his arguments really well.

Riley spotted Larry's parents in the audience and gave them a small smile. They looked so happy, so incredibly proud. They were beaming at Larry, and when they saw Riley, they smiled at her, too.

Good for him, Riley thought. Maybe we do have a chance to win this thing! But then she glanced offstage, into the wings. No Chloe. No Eric.

Where *are* they? Riley wondered. How can they debate us if they don't even listen to our arguments?

And then it hit her. Chloe was doing this on purpose.

What was she trying to say? That she could win the debate without even listening to Riley's side of the argument?

Riley felt her face grow hot. How could Chloe treat her this way? Hadn't they always been not just sisters but best friends as well?

Suddenly Larry was sitting beside her and nudging her. "Riley, it's your turn. Get up there," he said softly.

Riley stood and walked to the podium. She took out her notes. But she was shaking inside. Shaking with anger and hurt.

Even if Chloe wasn't part of the debate, she should be here for me, Riley thought.

They'd always shown up to support each other at school events. Somehow, not showing up was the meanest thing of all.

Larry cleared his throat to get Riley to start talking.

"As my partner has said..." she began. But using the word *partner* made her mind wander. Partners. Isn't that what sisters-who-are-best-friends are supposed to be?

"If a homeless person happens to fall asleep in the library, how can we say that's any different from a tired grandmother falling asleep in a public park?" Riley said. "This isn't really a crime...."

Just then, she saw Chloe enter the auditorium and slip into a seat near the exit.

Huh? What's she doing out there? Riley wondered. She should be backstage. Unless now she thinks she's *too good* to debate me.

Larry cleared his throat again.

Riley glanced down at her notes to find her place. "Um, as I was saying, this isn't a crime. A crime is when someone takes something that doesn't belong to them. Like if a homeless person borrowed a brand-new blouse from someone without asking permission first...now *that's* a crime...."

Behind her, Riley sort of heard Larry shuffling in his chair, but she ignored him. "After all," she went on, "let's face it. Homeless people can be as considerate as anyone else. For instance, I believe that if a homeless girl *had* a telephone, she would go out of her way to give the messages to family members when they got calls...."

Larry cleared his throat again, as if he was trying to get her attention.

What? Riley wondered. She glanced behind her to see what his problem was.

"Stick to the notes," Larry whispered.

Notes? Riley had forgotten about her notes. All she could think about was Chloe.

"It's totally unforgivable!" she blurted out without realizing it.

Then she saw the faces of the people in the audience. They were all staring at her as if they thought she should be hauled off to the funny farm—pronto!

For a moment, she was frozen. She couldn't move or speak. Tears welled up in her eyes, and her face felt hotter than ever.

"Riley?" Larry whispered. "Are you okay?"

She wasn't. She was making a total idiot out of herself!

"Just pretend everyone's sitting in their underwear," he whispered. He was trying to be helpful. Riley knew that. But instead she felt like even more of a fool.

"I have to go," Riley murmured. She turned and ran off the stage, down the backstage steps, and through to the hall outside the auditorium.

Then she dashed into the rest room and burst into tears.

How could she do this to me? Riley thought as she sobbed. It was all Chloe's fault—somehow. It had to be.

The door opened and Chloe rushed in.

"Oh, great! Now you're here!" Riley yelled at her, still crying.

"What's wrong?" Chloe asked.

"What's *wrong*?" Riley screamed. "I can't believe you even have to *ask* that question! You only borrowed my new top without asking and before I even got to wear it. You asked me to join the debate club then didn't pick me as your debate partner. I was waiting like a jerk for Alex because you didn't give me his phone message. You didn't tell me about Mom. And then you had the *nerve* to say Larry and I could never win this debate. I mean, I wanted to talk to you, but you were yelling at me like a maniac!"

Chloe nodded. "I'm sorry. Really—that was terrible.

I totally lost it that day," she said. "But I had reasons."

"Reasons?" Riley asked. "What reasons?"

"You wouldn't understand," Chloe said. "You've been so mad at me, you don't care what I've been going through."

Tears still streamed down Riley's face. "What you've been going through?" She repeated the words, but she didn't understand what Chloe meant. Was there something else? Something Riley didn't even know about?

"I've had stuff on my mind," Chloe explained. "That's why I was in such a bad mood that day. Besides, you didn't give *me* the phone message from Eric. So there."

"So there?" All at once, Riley couldn't help it—she started laughing. "Who says *so there*?"

As soon as she laughed, Chloe did, too.

Is that really all they were fighting about? Some phone messages and a shirt?

"Oh my gosh, I'm sorry," Riley said, wiping her tears and realizing what a fool she'd been.

"No, I*'m* sorry," Chloe said, stepping closer. "I didn't know you hadn't worn that top. There were no tags on it. And I didn't mean to forget about Alex's message. Then things just got out of control for me and I blew up at you. It wasn't fair."

"We should have just talked," Riley said. "Like Alex and Sierra and just about everyone else told me!"

Chloe nodded. "Why didn't you just tell me what was wrong?"

Riley shrugged. "Because we hardly *ever* fight. And I didn't want to start one over a stupid blouse. But then things just kept building, and I couldn't help it. I thought you were totally ignoring my feelings."

"No way. I'm all for getting the feelings out. I mean, it's not good to bottle them up," Chloe said. "And I'm pretty sure it's bad for your skin."

Riley laughed. "I hate being mad at you."

"Me, too," Chloe said. "You've got to promise that from now on when something's bothering you, you'll tell me. Okay?"

"Okay. I'll try," Riley said.

"Is there anything else on your mind?" Chloe said.

"No, it's all the stuff I just said. I mean, I guess the peasant blouse was the starter, but when you left me with Larry as a debate partner..."

"Oh, I'm so sorry about that," Chloe said. "But I didn't think we'd promised to be partners. And besides, Larry was awesome! I was listening from the back."

"I know," Riley admitted. "He really came through, didn't he? And then I messed it up." She blew her nose and then something occurred to her. "Hey, why didn't you and Eric debate, anyway?"

"Eric didn't show," Chloe explained. "No. I shouldn't say that. He withdrew us from the debate. Thank goodness! We would have bombed. We didn't even practice once!"

"How come? What's been going on with you?"

Chloe sighed. "I've wanted to tell you all about it all week," she said, suddenly talking really fast. "It's Mom. You know how her big show tomorrow is in trouble, right?"

Riley nodded.

"Well, I've been going crazy trying to help. So I never had time to work with Eric," Chloe admitted.

Riley listened as Chloe explained the whole thing. All about Tedi quitting. And how Chloe felt responsible. And how she'd been trying for days and days to get Tedi to come back.

"Wow. That's huge," Riley said. "I thought you were just shopping with Tedin. I had no idea you were trying to fix things."

"I've been going nuts!" Chloe moaned. "Nothing works!"

Then she explained about her plan to make Tedi hate her job by bringing some bratty kids to the photo studio.

"Hey, I know a *really* bratty kid," Riley offered. "Benji Slenkoff. He bites!"

"Cool!" Chloe said. "Do you think you could bring him to the mall tonight?"

"Definitely." Riley leaned over and gave her sister a big hug.

"I'm so glad we're not fighting anymore!" Chloe said.

"Me, too," Riley added.

so little time

It's so great to be able to talk things over with Chloe. I should have done it a long, long time ago, Riley realized.

Now that they were friends again, there wasn't anything they couldn't do!

chapter
twelve

Riley splashed her face with water in the rest room and then hurried to apologize to Larry.

"Hey, it's okay," he said, being as sweet as he always was. "I stepped up and finished your arguments for you."

"You did?" Riley was amazed.

Larry nodded. "I even threw in a line about how homeless people are no different from other people who've had problems sometimes and have had to leave the stage when they weren't feeling well. The audience loved it. And we won, since Chloe's team defaulted and didn't debate."

"Larry, you're the best!" Riley said.

His face spread into a huge grin. "I am? No, wait. *You're* the best. You helped me get over my fear."

Riley smiled at him, proud of herself. At least I did that much, she thought.

"Sierra and I are going out to celebrate my victory," Larry said. "I mean, our victory. You want to come?"

"I can't right now," Riley said. "I've got an emergency situation. But have a milk shake for me."

Chloe was waiting for Riley at the end of the hall. The two of them raced home and Riley called Benji Slenkoff's mom.

"Mrs. Slenkoff?" Riley said. She could hear Benji whining and shouting in the background. "How would you like me to take Benji to the mall to get his picture taken? For free. I mean, no baby-sitting charge."

Mrs. Slenkoff was so excited, she almost screamed. "Are you serious? Riley Carlson, I'm nominating you for sainthood!"

"Chloe and I will pick him in up fifteen minutes," Riley said before hanging up.

"This better work," Chloe said nervously. "I'm so worried about Mom."

"I know," Riley said. "If Tedi doesn't come back, she's going to have to use Bernadette the Sneezer."

When they got to Mrs. Slenkoff's house, Benji was in a bad mood.

"Hi, Benji," Riley said, bending down and trying to charm him. "Hey, guess what we're doing?"

He stuck out his tongue and spit at her.

"Excellent!" Chloe said, beaming. "This is going to be perfect!"

Mrs. Slenkoff glanced at Chloe. "Riley, is your sister feeling all right?" she asked.

Riley laughed. "Don't worry," she said. "We'll take

good care of Benji. And we'll have him back home by seven o'clock. Is that okay?"

"Is it okay? I could kiss you!" Mrs. Slenkoff said as she pressed some money into Riley's hands. "Here, take this. For the photos—and to get something to eat, too."

"I don't wanna go!" Benji whined.

But he didn't kick or scream, so Riley knew he wasn't going to put up much of a fight.

"Come on. It'll be fun. I'll let you spit in the fountain," she whispered, taking him by the hand.

[Riley: Everything I know about baby-sitting, I learned from Dana Waldhorn—the coolest baby-sitter in the world. She always wore awesome clothes, and she'd do Chloe's and my hair every time she came over. Then she'd let us try on all her makeup—even though we were really little and usually smashed the lipsticks. Dana's secret was simple. She totally got that a baby-sitter was not supposed to be a parent. As long as we were safe and the furniture wasn't destroyed, the rest was okay with her. Of course there's NO WAY I'm going to treat Benji the way Dana treated me. Nope. I'm not REALLY going to let him spit in the fountain. I want him in a BAD mood when he meets Tedi—not a good one. Duh!]

Riley tugged on Benji's hand. He's getting stronger, she thought as she sort of pulled him out of the house.

By the time they got to the mall, Tara and Quinn were already there. They had only one child with them—a little girl named Juliet. And the kid was smiling.

"What's up with her?" Chloe whispered to Tara. "I thought you said she was bratty."

"She's usually terrible," Tara whispered back, "but she loves me and she loves the mall."

It figures, Riley thought.

"I couldn't get the kids I usually sit for," Quinn explained. "They were going to a school play."

"Oh, well," Chloe said. "Where's Amanda?"

Quinn pointed behind them. "Here she comes now."

Riley turned around and saw Amanda striding toward them with a grumpy eight-year-old boy beside her. He was huge—almost as tall as Amanda was.

"Hey," Amanda said.

"Hey," Chloe whispered. "Who's that? Are we supposed to get his picture taken with the babies?"

Amanda leaned forward so the kid wouldn't hear her. "It's Max. He's grown since I sat for him a few months ago. I think he shot up about four inches."

"This is dumb." Max spoke up. "I thought you said we were going to the arcade."

"We will," Amanda promised him. "But we have to get your picture taken first."

"Oh, man!" the kid complained. "That stuff's for babies!"

Riley wanted to grin, but she tried not to let it show.

Let's see Tedi handle *him*! she thought. She shot Chloe a glance, and Chloe nodded. Yeah. This could be good.

"Okay, let's go," Chloe said, leading the way to the photo studio.

Luckily, it was a slow night at the mall, so they didn't have to wait. Tedi was standing around with nothing to do.

"Hi, stranger!" Riley said, giving Tedi a hug. "So you've got a new job, huh?"

Tedi nodded. "Yeah. It's all good," she said, but Riley thought she heard a note of good-but-getting-boring in Tedi's voice.

"So we brought you some customers!" Chloe said cheerfully.

"Yes, I see," Tedi replied.

"I'm not doing this," Max declared, shaking his head and backing away.

Hee-hee, Riley thought. Way to go, Max!

"Hey, you don't have to get your picture taken if you don't want to," Tedi said, turning on her charm. "How about helping me with the lights instead?"

Max shrugged, looking happier. "Sure. Why not?" he said.

"Oh, no, Tedi, we need to get his picture taken," Amanda insisted. "I promised his mom."

Tedi leaned close to Amanda and whispered, "Don't worry. I'll get it later."

Wow, Riley thought. She's smart! She's not going to

push him but will let him feel comfortable, and then she'll sneak it in later somehow. No wonder she doesn't want to go back to modeling. She's really good at this job!

Chloe gave Riley a worried look.

Riley was worried, too. The bratty kids weren't being very bratty. And Tedi seemed to be used to it, anyway.

Okay, Riley thought. Let's have Benji do his thing.

"Benji, you go first," Riley said, yanking him a little to put him in an even worse mood.

"I don't wanna!" he whined. But he got up on the posing stand without much of an argument.

Tedi turned on a smile for him. "Hey, Benji," she said. "You want a red background for your picture or a blue one?"

"Blue," he said.

"Perfect," Tedi said, since the blue background was already in place.

She stepped behind the camera and focused it. Then she snapped her fingers to show him where to look.

"Ready?" Tedi said. "I'll count to three. One... two...three!"

On three, she clicked the shutter and the lights flashed.

But Benji had stuck out his tongue at the last instant and made a face.

Tedi laughed. "Okay, you got me," she said. "Let's do it again."

"I don't wanna!" Benji whined again.

"Is that the brattiest he gets?" Chloe muttered.

"No," Riley whispered back. "I told you! He usually bites me!"

Chloe shook her head, and Riley closed her eyes.

Come on, Benji, Riley silently prayed. At least he could kick or throw something!

"Ready?" Tedi said. "One...two...three!"

On three, he made a face again.

Yes! Riley thought.

But Tedi wasn't upset. She actually laughed!

"Ha, ha," Tedi said good-naturedly. "You got me again. Okay, one more time." She stood behind the camera with a twinkle in her eye.

And Benji had a devilish look in his eyes.

But Tedi was smarter. She clicked the shutter on "one" instead of "three" and got a decent picture of him.

"I want to go spit in the fountain!" Benji shouted.

"No way," Riley said. "You haven't been bad enough."

"Huh?" Tedi said. "Don't you mean he hasn't been good enough?"

Oops! Riley thought. "Yeah, that's it," she said quickly.

Next, Tedi took two really cute portraits of Juliet. Then it was Max's turn.

"I've got a baseball background," she said, seeing Max's baseball shirt. "You want to pose like a pitcher?"

"Yeah," Max said, grinning. "Okay. That would be cool."

Tedi grinned triumphantly and shot Riley a glance that said, *See? I told you I'd get him to cooperate!*

Riley and Chloe watched glumly and silently.

The plan wasn't working—at all. It was a complete bust!

Tedi wasn't a bit unhappy with her job. Why should she be? She was fantastic at it!

"What are we going to do?" Riley asked Chloe when they had finally taken all the kids home and were back in their own room.

"What can we do?" Chloe replied. "Mom's going to have to use Bernadette the Sneezer."

Riley cringed. She could see it now: drippy marks all over the silk gowns.

"All we can do is show up at the show tomorrow and give Mom our support," Chloe said.

"Yeah," Riley said. "She's going to need it."

chapter
thirteen

"**W**here is she?" Chloe asked Manuelo outside the Palace Hotel ballroom the next day after school.

She and Riley had taken two buses to get to the fashion show in time, before Macy's collection was presented.

"Your mother? She's backstage," Manuelo said, rushing away frantically. "You'd better hurry if you want to see her before her collection goes on."

"Is she freaking?" Riley asked.

Manuelo didn't answer. He had run off to help someone find the press kits for all the reporters who were there.

The place was buzzing, and Chloe felt a jolt of excitement. She'd seen other fashion shows but never such a big one.

Two ballrooms had been opened up to connect with each other. The whole space was darkened and filled with folding chairs on each side of the runway. Colored spotlights were aimed at the middle. And a television crew was set up in back, taping the whole thing.

Loud, pulsing rock music with a heavy beat filled the air.

"Let's find Mom," Riley said.

Chloe nodded and followed.

They walked down the hall to a third, smaller, adjoining ballroom. It was being used as a backstage area, with dressing rooms for all the models and designers.

Inside, the place was packed. Makeup tables and racks of clothes were everywhere. All the designers were rushing around like crazy, grabbing clothes and giving orders.

"This is so exciting!" Chloe said.

"Yeah, but where's Mom?" Riley wondered out loud.

They made their way through a crowded space where the models were having their makeup done. Or slipping into tiny skirts. Or standing still while someone messed up their hair—perfectly.

"I've never seen so many beautiful women in one spot in my life," Chloe said.

"I've never seen so much lip gloss!" Riley joked.

Then Chloe rounded a corner and caught sight of Bernadette in the long cream-colored silk gown.

"Oh my gosh!" Riley cried in horror.

"What?" Chloe asked.

Riley pointed. "Look!"

They both stared at Bernadette, who was a total mess. Her eyes and nose were red and puffy from sneezing. But her face, neck, and arms were the worst. She was completely broken out in hives!

Chloe clapped a hand over her mouth just as Bernadette sneezed.

"Ahhhhhh-choooooo!"

"This is a total nightmare!" Chloe whispered to her sister.

"What can we do?" Riley said.

"I don't know. Nothing." Chloe bit her nail. "I'll bet Mom's totally out of her mind."

Riley approached the model, although she couldn't get too close because Bernadette kept sneezing. "Bernadette, what's happening?" she asked. "I mean, are you sick? You aren't even holding any flowers."

"I found out I'm allergic to si-si-si-silk!" she said as she sneezed again.

"Silk!" Chloe's eyes popped open wide. "But almost everything in Mom's collection is made of silk!"

Riley handed Bernadette a tissue and stood back. The girl looked like she was about to sneeze again.

"I guess we just have to be ready to watch Mom totally fall apart," Chloe said. "It's a good thing we came to support her."

A moment later Macy breezed into the part of the dressing room where Chloe and Riley were standing. "Oh, hi, sweeties," she said. "I'm so glad you're here."

Huh? Chloe did a double take. Was her mom actually smiling?

[Chloe: Let me explain something here. My mom is never—and I mean NEVER—calm at her fashion shows. I mean, she once totally freaked out when a model wore a wristwatch upside down at a show. And it was a tiny little watch, the size of a dime. Like anyone in the audience was going to notice that those itty-bitty numbers were facing the wrong way. I'm just saying she gets crazy about this stuff pretty easily. So can someone please explain why she's as cool as a cucumber when her main model is a sneezing, sniffling mess?]

"Don't you want to get seats out front?" Macy said. "My designs are on in about ten minutes."

Chloe started to answer, but Bernadette sneezed again.

"Oh, for heaven's sake," Macy said, whirling around. "Will someone please help the girl out of that dress?"

"Mom, what's going on?" Riley said. "Bernadette's a wreck! Why aren't you?"

Macy laughed. "Well, that's because..." she started to say.

But then Chloe and Riley both saw the answer.

Tedi was there!

She was standing near a lighted mirror, having her

makeup done. Macy's beautiful ice-blue gown looked absolutely stunning on her. So did the little silver flat shoes.

"Tedi!" Chloe said, racing up to her. "What happened? I thought you wanted to be an average, ordinary person."

"Oh, being average is so twenty minutes ago," Tedi said. "I mean, I liked working at the mall, and the kids were great. But I *love* modeling."

Duh! Chloe thought.

"Tedi called me last night," Macy explained. "We finally had a heart-to-heart talk."

"Right," Tedi said. "Talking is everything. We solved all our problems."

Duh again, Chloe thought.

"I promised not to work Tedi so hard," Macy admitted. "I mean, I guess everyone needs a little time at the beach—even if salt water and sun *are* bad for your hair! And Tedi promised never to quit like that again!"

Wow, Chloe thought. That's so great.

"Well, go get seats, girls," Macy said. "The show is about to begin!"

"This is awesome!" Riley cried as they hurried into the ballroom.

The lights in the ballroom dimmed and Macy's show began. Tedi looked amazing. And the crowd went wild for the designs!

"Hey, I have an idea," Chloe whispered. "Next time

there's a debate, let's be partners for sure. Okay?"

"That works for me," Riley said. "And I know what the topic of our debate should be," she added with a grin. "Let's argue for the major importance of girl talk!"

Chloe smiled back at her sister. She was so happy that they were best friends again, and she was thrilled that everything had worked out between Mom and Tedi as well.

"Yeah," she agreed. "Girl talk definitely rocks!"

mary-kate olsen ashley olsen

so little time

Chloe
and Riley's

SCRAPBOOK

Here's a sneak peek at

so little time

Book 8
the love factor

Chloe nodded, her hands fluttering under the table. This was terrible! She couldn't talk. She couldn't think. Her head was an ice cap.

"Hey," Lennon said, pausing at their table. "How's it going?"

Chloe lifted a hand in a flat wave. She pressed the other hand against her nose. "Owwwww!"

Lennon folded his arms. "Chloe? Are you okay?"

"She'll be fine," Riley explained quickly. "It's a brain freeze."

"Brain freeze?" Lennon laughed. "Yeah, I sometimes have that effect on people. I freak them out. They get intimidated by my incredible wealth of knowledge."

Oh, give me a break! Chloe wanted to shout. But she could only work on thawing her head.

"Brain freeze. Ha!" Lennon said, moving over toward a group of guys.

Riley gave Chloe a sympathetic look. "Is that the worst timing or what? Your big chance with Lennon and your whole head ices over!"

"My fault," Chloe said in a mousy voice. She shivered. "Why do I let myself go near anything with ice?"

She spotted Alex Zimmer across the room, sneaking up behind Riley. He squeezed Riley's shoulders. "Guess what? I have great news," he announced.

Riley turned around and smiled at him.

Alex's dark eyes sparkled with excitement. "We have a gig for this weekend. Friday night at Mango's!"

"What?" Sierra cried. She and Alex played together in a band called The Wave. "This weekend? No way!"

Alex nodded proudly. "I just talked to the manager and we're on for Friday night. It's a solid break for the band."

"That's fantastic!" Riley said, nudging Alex's arm.

As they talked out the details, Chloe turned to the coffee bar looking for Lennon. Her embarrassment was melting with her brain freeze. Now she just felt a burning challenge. She wanted to ask him out. She wanted to get an up-close and personal look at Mr. Know-it-All. And she wanted to prove that she wasn't afraid of him.

"I'd better tell Saul," Alex said, taking out his cell phone to call the band's drummer. "He'll probably want to pull together a rehearsal this afternoon."

"There's no way I can rehearse today," Sierra said, disappointed. "I have to head home."

"No problem," Alex told her. "I just want to try out a new song. If it works, you can learn it later in the week." Then he turned to Riley and flipped his phone closed. "Oh, Riley! I almost forgot. We were supposed to hang out this afternoon."

"No, it's okay," Riley replied.

"We really need to rehearse," Alex said. "But I was looking forward to seeing you."

"No problem," Riley said. "I totally understand. Friday night is going to be great."

"Hey, Riley," Larry said. "Since you're not hanging with Alex this afternoon, that means you're free! You can come surfing with me!"

"Surfing?" Riley blinked.

Chloe smothered a laugh. Surfing with Larry was not Riley's idea of a great afternoon.

"Well, you said that you always wanted to try it," Larry pointed out.

"Go for it!" Sierra said as she hitched up her backpack. "You like to try new things. And Malibu has some of the best surfing in the world."

Riley turned to Larry in his fire-engine-red wetsuit.

"It's the coolest!" Larry jumped onto a chair and struck a pose, arms out, as if riding a wave. "Let's ride the swells, Shred Betty!" he said.

Riley winced up at Larry's glowing red suit. "I guess…"

"Awesome! Let's go!" Larry said, tugging Riley out of her chair. "We don't want to be late."

Suddenly, Chloe felt a new panic. Everyone was leaving! Alex headed toward the door with his phone pressed to his ear. Larry dragged Riley. Sierra dragged her violin case.

"Hey, guys! Wait! You can't leave me here!" Chloe cried.

"Then come with us!" Riley said.

Chloe hurried over to Riley and Sierra. "Don't leave me here alone. Lennon will think I'm a loser."

"But I thought you didn't like him," Riley said.

"I think I changed my mind," Chloe said. "I'm going to make a move. Soon."

"Gotta go," Sierra said, ducking out.

"Sorry!" Riley called as Larry tugged her toward the door. "Good luck!"

That left Chloe to scurry back to the table alone. Grabbing her copy of *Teen Spree*, she leaned back in the chair. Look relaxed, she thought. Be cool. A girl glanced at her and Chloe smiled back as if to say: I have got it all together.

The page was still open to the Love Factor quiz. Chloe brightened. How perfect! She could take the quiz for Lennon and her. She pulled out a purple pen and dug in. She answered question one and checked her score. The highest score possible. She answered questions two and three, then checked the answer key.

Another great score!

Chloe's heart beat fast with excitement. She and

Lennon were totally perfect for each other. She couldn't wait to finish the quiz! With a secret smile, she looked around for Lennon. There he was, sliding his folded apron onto the coffee bar. He had his backpack on and…

Oh, no! He was leaving. His shift was ending. She had to grab him before it was too late!

Chloe dropped her pen and hurried over to the coffee bar. Forget about acting casual. This was her chance to get a date with the perfect boy for her.

Trying to pretend she wasn't nervous, she squeezed in next to Lennon at the counter. "Hey, Lennon," she said.

Lennon turned away from the cappuccino machine and smiled at her. "Brain freeze over?"

"I'm totally thawed," Chloe said. Then she thought of an angle. "I didn't see you at the last party at the senior center."

"I had to go to a wedding with my parents," Lennon said.

"Hey, Lennon," one of his friends called. "Over here."

"In a minute," Lennon called, turning back to Chloe.

She was close enough to see the tiny flecks of blue in his gray eyes. Those eyes…

"My friends are waiting," he said.

Chloe nodded. Enough small talk, she thought. Time to pop the big Q. "So I just found out my friend Sierra is playing at Mango's," she said.

"Really?" Lennon seemed interested.

"With her band, The Wave." Chloe's heart was beating hard in her chest. She wanted to do the safe thing and stop right now, but she plunged on. "They're performing this Friday night," Chloe said, bracing herself. "And I…"

Just then, someone turned on the cappuccino machine. *Whirrrrr!*

It drowned out Chloe's words: "…I *was wondering if you'd like to go with me?*"

Lennon squinted, his eyes on Chloe's lips as if he was trying to read them.

Did he hear me? she wondered when the machine stopped.

Lennon nodded slowly. "That's cool," he said.

"Hey, Lennon!" his friend called again.

"Look, I have to go," Lennon said. "But we'll talk later."

"Right," Chloe said. She smiled, trying to cover her confusion as Lennon headed off. She replayed the scene in her head as she went back to her table.

Okay, she got bonus points for asking Lennon out.

The only problem was…she wasn't sure if he'd heard her. Did she have a date for Friday night or not?

WIN A MARY-KATE AND ASHLEY
Secret Crush Prize Pack!

....

TWENTY LUCKY WINNERS WILL RECEIVE:

20 GRAND PRIZE WINNERS!

- A **CRUSH COURSE** videogame

- **Cool journal and pen**

- **Stationery from the** *mary-kateandashley* **brand**

- **Lip gloss from the** *mary-kateandashley* **brand**

- **An autographed copy of**
so little time #6 : Secret Crush

SO LITTLE TIME
Secret Crush Prize Pack Sweepstakes

OFFICIAL RULES:

1. No purchase necessary.

2. To enter complete the official entry form or hand print your name, address, age, and phone number along with the words "SO LITTLE TIME Secret Crush Prize Pack Sweepstakes" on a 3" x 5" card and mail to: SO LITTLE TIME Secret Crush Prize Pack Sweepstakes, c/o HarperEntertainment, Attn: Children's Marketing Department, 10 East 53rd Street, New York, NY 10022. Entries must be received no later than April 30, 2003. Enter as often as you wish, but each entry must be mailed separately. One entry per envelope. Partially completed, illegible, or mechanically reproduced entries will not be accepted. Sponsors are not responsible for lost, late, mutilated, illegible, stolen, postage due, incomplete, or misdirected entries. All entries become the property of Dualstar Entertainment Group, LLC, and will not be returned.

3. Sweepstakes open to all legal residents of the United States (excluding Colorado and Rhode Island) who are between the ages of five and fifteen on April 30, 2003, excluding employees and immediate family members of HarperCollins Publishers, Inc. ("HarperCollins"), Parachute Properties and Parachute Press, Inc., and their respective subsidiaries and affiliates, officers, directors, shareholders, employees, agents, attorneys, and other representatives (individually and collectively "Parachute"), Dualstar Entertainment Group, LLC, and its subsidiaries and affiliates, officers, directors, shareholders, employees, agents, attorneys, and other representatives (individually and collectively "Dualstar"), and their respective parent companies, affiliates, subsidiaries, advertising, promotion and fulfillment agencies, and the persons with whom each of the above are domiciled. Offer void where prohibited or restricted by law.

4. Odds of winning depend on the total number of entries received. Approximately 225,000 sweepstakes announcements published. All prizes will be awarded. Winners will be randomly drawn on or about May 15, 2003, by HarperEntertainment, whose decisions are final. Potential winners will be notified by mail and will be required to sign and return an affidavit of eligibility and release of liability within 14 days of notification. Prizes won by minors will be awarded to parent or legal guardian who must sign and return all required legal documents. By acceptance of their prize, winners consent to the use of their names, photographs, likeness, and personal information by HarperCollins, Parachute, Dualstar, and for publicity purposes without further compensation except where prohibited.

5. Twenty (20) Grand Prize Winners will win a Secret Crush Prize Pack which includes the following: a *Crush Course* videogame; a journal; pen; stationery; lip gloss; and an autographed SO LITTLE TIME: SECRET CRUSH book. Sponsor reserves the right to substitute another prize of equal or greater value in the event that the winner is unable to receive the prize for any reason. Approximate retail value per prize: $70.00.

6. Only one prize will be awarded per individual, family, or household. Prizes are non-transferable and cannot be sold or redeemed for cash. No cash substitute is available. Any federal, state, or local taxes are the responsibility of the winner. Sponsor may substitute prize of equal or greater value, if necessary, due to availability.

7. Additional terms: By participating, entrants agree a) to the official rules and decisions of the judges, which will be final in all respects; and to waive any claim to ambiguity of the official rules and b) to release, discharge, and hold harmless HarperCollins, Parachute, Dualstar, and their affiliates, subsidiaries, and advertising and promotion agencies from and against any and all liability or damages associated with acceptance, use, or misuse of any prize received in this sweepstakes.

8. Any dispute arising from this Sweepstakes will be determined according to the laws of the State of New York, without reference to its conflict of law principles, and the entrants consent to the personal jurisdiction of the State and Federal courts located in New York County and agree that such courts have exclusive jurisdiction over all such disputes.

9. To obtain the name of the winners, please send your request and a self-addressed stamped envelope (excluding residents of Vermont and Washington) to SO LITTLE TIME Secret Crush Prize Pack Sweepstakes Winners, c/o HarperEntertainment, Attn: Children's Marketing Department, 10 East 53rd Street, New York, NY 10022 by June 1, 2003. Sweepstakes Sponsor: HarperCollins Publishers, Inc.

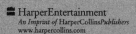

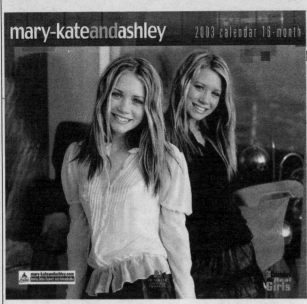